The Fingers of the Colossus

Ten Short Stories

KEITH SOARES

Bufflegoat Books

Special thanks to Layla for putting up with all this writing silliness and for help with this book. Additional thanks to Bill Setzer and Christopher Durso.

Also from Keith Soares

The Oasis of Filth
Part 1: The Oasis of Filth
Part 2: The Hopeless Pastures
Part 3: From Blood Reborn

Fogland: The Twelfth Quay of Water Street

The Fingers of the Colossus (Ten Short Stories)

John Black series
For I Could Lift My Finger and Black Out the Sun
Part 1: DAWN
Part 2: MORN [Forthcoming]
Part 3: NOON [Forthcoming]
Part 4: EVEN [Forthcoming]
Part 5: DUSK [Forthcoming]

THE FINGERS OF THE COLOSSUS

The Space Between

The tiny dot flickered, tugging at my vision, but lost again in an instant. CCC was reporting nothing. The wide fabric of darkness was littered with tiny dots, varying in sizes, colors. A field of hazy lightness wrapped around like a distant scarf, but utterly cold.

I studied the view from one side to the other, scanning for *something*. The wide windows of Observation showed me everything. And nothing. And that was the problem.

It was six days since Maria and Victor died. Four since Oleg. And just one since Jenk. And... him. There were enough supplies to last me maybe ten more days, and that was a stretch. Seven days was more likely.

The sun... the goddamned sun. Brightest thing out there, and yet I know all too well exactly what it was hiding. At this Lagrangian point, Sun-Earth L3, I was directly on the opposite side of the sun from home, Earth. That meant no direct line of sight, no direct communications. I was on an island on the wrong side of space.

Artemis said he had no choice. What the hell did I know, I'm just the purser. I barely remember any training on how to run this big hunk of metal. And in any event, the ship was floating dead; out of fuel. Artemis used the last to park us at L3. He said at least that way we wouldn't just drift away in the *wrong* direction, at least for a while, until the complex gravitational tug of the orbiting planets pulled us some way or another. But then things got worse.

Hell of a purser I was. All my crates blown out to space. Low on food, I searched every nook looking for more. What I found would last a week, if I starved myself. More importantly, the water is low. Really low. Must've been hit, too. Damn it.

The only crates not floating in space were marked 'SCIENTIFIC,' to be held for Dr. Luthra. I figured she didn't mind if I cracked those open. She was one of the first to die at the hands of the other doctor, the medical one. Raskin. Besides, if I die not realizing that there was salvation hiding in one of these boxes, I'm going to feel like a real schmuck for an eternity of after-life.

One in a million. In the universe, you know, those are pretty damn good odds. If the odds of human life evolving were one in a million, there'd be 30,000 planets full of people *in the Milky Way alone*. But when they tell you a certain mishap has million-to-one odds, you sort of forget about the vastness of space, and just think *oh, that sounds pretty safe*. Well, I don't know if the odds were one in a million, one in a billion or whatever. All I know is that it happened.

A hail of micrometeroids pierced the ship in several places, the most severe in the Med Bay. Dr. Raskin was there and should've had alarms all around him blaring, but defying those long odds, one of the little things took out the air pressure gauges for that sector. Single point of failure. Stupid.

And Raskin, invariably scratching his scraggly beard, was busy trying to put Mike back together after a drill tore him up. Mike was screaming so loud that I could hear him all the way in Storage, at least until Raskin knocked him out with something. But Mike's leg was a ragged mess, so Raskin kept working on it as best he could, assisted by Majel. The two were in the Med Bay for hours as the air seeped out and the pressure dropped.

Then Majel complained of unbearable pain in her left shoulder, and suddenly Raskin had two patients. He made the obligatory CCC log entry, so on a ship our size the news spread fast: two down. Normally, I think, Majel's pain would've been enough warning to make Raskin understand that it was decompression sickness. But by then, I guess, his mind may already have been altered. Where she had bubbles in her shoulder joint, he had them in his brain.

The rest of us paid no attention to Med Bay. We didn't know how to help, figured they had it under control, and besides there were alarms going off in four other sections, including mine. In Storage, I used a handheld sensor/smoker to find the pinholes in the hull, plugged them up with high-grade patches, turned off the alarm.

Meanwhile, other holes got punched into two of our four fuel tanks. They held for a while, as Artemis and Jenk no doubt planned an EVA to try to fix them, but then an explosion took out Gamma and carried over to Delta. The hull remained intact, miraculously, but the claw was damaged enough that the asteroid we'd been mining slipped away. After a while, that asteroid was just one more tiny dot in the darkness. We floated our separate ways. I guess that was sort of lucky. Tank Alpha had been empty for weeks; Beta was down to less than a third. That remainder plus the emergency reserves were what we used to fly to our little space parking spot. We all thought it might be the last place we'd ever see in this lifetime. At the least, most of us were right.

"Just the purser." I heard people say it behind my back all the time. Well, here it may have saved my life. Dr. Raskin killed Majel and Mike while they were both lying on his own med gurneys. Sedated them until their hearts stopped. After we parked at L3, Raskin made a call to Artemis; told him to bring Dr. Luthra, Jenk, everyone else, too. Something he needed to show us. Artemis stayed with protocol, left the Conn in Jenk's hands and gathered up only Luthra, in the lab. As they entered Med Bay, Raskin hit Artemis in the head, hard. That killed him instantly, though it was really messy. Then he came for Dr. Luthra. She was maybe 45 kilos,

Raskin was much bigger. When it happened I was deep in Storage, but the scream sounded like it was right next to me. I remember that scream.

Victor and Oleg, the drillers, were big guys. Raskin considered their reaction to the sound of a woman screaming, imagined they'd try to be heroes. Raskin was crazy now, but the son of a bitch was smart. Crafty. Devious. And all that meant dangerous. Raskin did a complete lockdown of Med Bay, and as chief med officer, there was nothing a couple of drillers could do but pound on sealed doors and look through thick windows.

I was summoned to the Conn as the drillers shared what they found with the remaining crew, all of it entered into the CCC logs. Raskin had turned off his lights, but drillers carry tools. With their own torches, they had enough light to see what remained of Artemis and Luthra through the small portal. They couldn't see Mike or Majel, but since no one answered their shouts and door pounding they assumed the worst. Then Raskin blocked the view.

Just like that, our captain, science officer, medical assistant and one of our drillers were dead. And our chief medical officer had gone violently insane. Bad day in space.

That left our second, two more drillers, our cook, and... me. Four dead, six alive. One nuts.

Jenk was a good guy, probably would've made a good commander one day, but thrust into command and instantly dealing with what was probably the biggest man-made catastrophe in human spaceflight history, he looked green as new mown grass. He sat thinking, like the wheels were turning but no cogs were catching. Maria, the cook, was terrified. Victor and Oleg wanted blood.

I just thought how this space mission was turning out a lot different than I'd planned. I'd always talked about how this trip was supposed to be a huge pay day, and then I was getting the hell out of the space mining business. I'd have enough for a place in West Virginia, maybe at the foot of some little mountain, a running brook along the house. I was going to spend all summer chopping wood and all winter burning it. A boy can dream. Now I was on a dead spacecraft further from home than any other ship I knew of, with a psychotic doctor killing the crew. One in a million.

Jenk used CCC to lock Med Bay on the outside as well, trying to seal the mad doctor in his own house of horrors. That gave us time to think. Getting home was top prio and Jenk was trying to connect the communications dots to make that happen. He was on the radio endlessly. Being opposite Earth and not at all where we were expected to be was a problem, but Artemis had called in our distress via long range just after it happened. We all knew that was our only hope.

Even in the face of disaster, you have to sleep. We all eventually shifted out of rotation, though Jenk kept on the radio. After tense hours of nothing happening, Maria and Victor went to get some sleep; Oleg and I stayed in the Conn with Jenk.

While they slept, that clever bastard Raskin used CCC to vent air from the Sleeper box. It was Central Computer Control, after all, not just run from the Conn. Maria and Victor were dead, asphyxiated, and we didn't even know it. Raskin shut off the alarms.

Oh, and he let himself out. Apparently Raskin knew a bit more about CCC security overrides than Jenk, or any of us for that matter. Like I said, Jenk looked green. It was almost laughable if it weren't so serious.

Oleg started preparations. The bastard had killed two of his fellow drillers, not to mention the others. In Oleg's mind, Raskin was less than dirt. Time to sweep the floor. The biggest drill was embedded into the hull of the ship on the outside. But there were smaller, mobile drill suits, and as Mike would attest, they could tear a man up.

We knew we'd need rest, but we no longer trusted the Sleeper box. Instead, we held the Conn, and used a few crates from Storage — the ones marked 'SCIENTIFIC' — to block open the main passages in all directions. If Raskin sucked out the air, he'd likely kill himself, too. It was low-tech, but it worked.

Jenk tried to get Oleg to consider a more thoughtful approach. Negotiate surrender, rather than frontal assault. Oleg was a big muscle-head, but even he could see the truth. We were stranded, we had no idea if there was a chance for rescue, and he wanted revenge. He thought for a day, then decided that if he was going down, he was going down swinging. Donning his mid-range drill suit, Oleg headed for the Med Bay. Jenk held the Conn and warned me to stay out of it, too. We're not military, so the only thing we had to fear from corporate was to be fired. But I played it cool while Oleg ran hot. I waited.

Oleg found that the door was locked, inside was dark. He banged on the door a bit for good measure, but he wasn't there to knock. He fired up the drill and laid into the large hinges beside the sealed door. Sparks flew and scraps of metal twisted into and out of the drill bit, falling away nearly molten hot. We watched Oleg from our CCC monitors. In his bulky suit, he stepped back as the door fell hard on the floor, echoing a heavy *boom*. Throughout the ship, we felt the reverberation.

A smell flowed out of Med Bay and spoke to what was in store. Dead things were waiting in the darkness. Oleg poked his madly spinning drill into the center of the opening, daring Raskin to try to slip by. Then he stepped forward and into Med Bay, swiping the deadly spinning drill from side to side. He pulled one hand out of the suit and reached over to the wall, slapping the switches to turn on the lights.

Inside, he saw the carnage, the remains of Artemis and Luthra. Artemis had the back of his skull caved in and laid face-down in the middle of the floor in the receiving pod, a wide pool of blood drying around him. Luthra had backed to a wall before cowering in fear in front of Raskin. The same heavy tool that had caved in Artemis' skull still protruded from Luthra's forehead, the rest of her face frozen in a permanent scream of terror. Blood and gore was all over the room, splattered by the vicious attacks. On the monitor, we could see Oleg pause. It was a gruesome sight. Then he stepped toward the back and Recovery. He peeked in to see the still forms of Majel and Mike. The radio crackled faintly.

"He's not here," Oleg reported in thickly Russian-accented English.

Jenk stared at the monitor. After a pause, he responded.

"Are you sure?"

On screen, Oleg's form slowly turned left then right, scanning. "Da. I'm sure."

Then he tensed. He heard something behind him, but the big drill suit couldn't turn fast enough. A figure in a light green lab coat raced through the Med Bay door and leapt onto his back. Reaching into the unprotected rear of the drill suit and wielding a portable laser scalpel, Raskin cut Oleg nearly in half as the big Russian let out a hellish scream. As one, they spun and tumbled to the floor. The wildly spinning drill tore into a gurney, shredding it and sending pieces flying before digging into the floor itself. Oleg tried to pull the drill out and turn it toward his attacker, but already in shock from the pain and loss of blood, it was too late. Raskin pried himself from the back of the suit and stood up. As the last life fled from Oleg, his grip on the drill trigger faded and the turning bit slowed, then stopped. The metallic chewing noises ceased and the entire ship was eerily quiet.

Raskin turned and looked directly into the camera with wild, bloodshot eyes. For a moment, he scratched his beard, like he was considering what to do. Then he ran off out of view.

"Damn it!" Jenk slammed his hand down on the console arm. "Computer! Hall 6 camera!" he shouted. He quickly tapped keys and on-screen controls to speed the changing views, but one by one the cameras on board were going dark. Jenk's eyes grew wide, as he turned and looked at me. I said nothing, barely making eye contact. I was just the purser. I had no idea what to do.

He muttered something about protocol and tapped over to the Conn manuals. Zipping through text on screen, I had no idea what he was looking for. Seemed to me that we had a problem here and now, and some arcane text in CCC was unlikely to help. Unless of course there was a manual segment on dealing with catastrophic crew loss at the hands of a murderously insane medical officer. I was never one for memorizing protocol, but I was willing to bet that chapter had been left out.

Raskin. Jenk. Me. The remaining crew of the IMES *Victory*.

I'd always loved that our ship had such a positive and uplifting name: *Victory!* Made me wonder if anyone at Command bothered to look up either of the ancient British naval ships named HMS *Victory*, both of which met their doom in tragic accidents. Well, I guess we fit right in.

* * *

I've been here, just waiting, for days now. I don't have many days left. Waking up on the floor in the middle of Observation, I recall everything that happened as I scan the dark for a sign, any sign. I've eaten the last of my food. Water is down under half a liter. But that tiny dot flickered again. Still, CCC made no reports.

After Oleg died, Raskin disappeared. Jenk and I stayed in the Conn, taking shifts to stand guard. Jenk took one PCL — personal comm link — and gave me another. I asked why, since we were in the same room. He said it was protocol in situations where crew members might be separated. I didn't argue, just took off my blue uniform shirt and pinned the PCL to my undershirt.

With crates blocking open our doors, we kept ourselves from being secretly asphyxiated, but left ourselves open to a direct assault from three sides. We were a mining ship so we had nothing in terms of traditional weapons. Jenk asked me for thoughts on what to use for self-defense. I considered what I had in Storage, all sorts of tools. In the end, I made a dash, terrified the whole way there and back, and chose the sealant catabolizer because it had a big warning label on it saying not to aim it at any life form. It instantly turned crate sealant into vapor and heat. If it did the same to a person, game over.

The layout of the Conn allowed one of us to have a prime view over the three doors leading to Halls 1, 2 and 3, as the other slept behind the console. We overlapped waking hours slightly, and always that time was spent eating while Jenk repeated his distress calls over the radio. Even though he had set CCC to report any incoming transmission in any language, as well as any ship sighting, I heard him continuously using the radio when it was my turn to sleep.

In my dreams, I saw the doctor's lunatic eyes. More than once I startled awake, expecting to see him standing over me.

Over the course of two days, Raskin actually did make an appearance, one time. He just stood in the dim green light down Hall 1, the one on our left that went toward Storage. I assumed this was a warning not to make any trips that direction again. He just stared at us as Jenk pushed me forward, with the catabolizer humming in my hand. Raskin looked directly into my eyes, then looked down at the device I held, assessing it.

"What's that?" he asked, rubbing that damned beard again. The sudden sound of his raspy voice startled me.

I puffed myself up a bit and glanced down at the thick tubular device. "Sealant catabolizer," I said, trying to sound calm and assured. I found myself scratching at my own face, where my own beard was now coming in. Hadn't shaved since things went south.

He laughed. Then I did too, I don't know why. We both laughed a minute, each scratching our faces like mirror images of each other. The whole damn thing was funny. I felt like I was acting a part, living another man's life. Like I was seeing through his eyes and he through mine. It was a joke. I thought for a moment that maybe I was losing my mind, too.

"Catabolizer. Clever of you. Breaks down molecules. Rather deadly, I'd say. Hmm… I wouldn't want to be on the wrong end of that," he finally said. Then he dipped his chin to glare at me. "I doubt you would either."

After a moment, he turned and disappeared.

* * *

Of all the things that've happened to me, I think this is the worst: I just spilled the last water. In desperation, I've been lapping it off the floor. But it's gone now. I haven't seen that flickering dot in a while. Maybe I just imagined it. Maybe that's why CCC hasn't said anything.

Another day and night passed, and the routine of being crammed in the Conn all day with nothing to do was already driving us stir crazy. I started to get rather sick of hearing Jenk on the radio, saying the same stupid things over and over with no hope of response. CCC was thankfully quiet. Mostly I just grew to hate the smell of being stuck there with Jenk for days on end. Thankfully there was a head off the back of the Conn that we could get to without exploring the darker parts of the ship, and we had food and water for several days in a small hold nearby. After that ran out, we'd have to go to Storage or just sit there and die. There was a lot of food and water in Storage. Was.

Raskin must've watched our patterns. One sleeping, the other watching. Both of us — hell, maybe *all three of us* — getting bored. The first two times we retrieved food and water from the small hold, I stood watch with the catabolizer while Jenk rushed in and out. It was just down Hall 2, dead center in front of the console.

Then I made a mistake.

A fatal mistake.

For Jenk, that is.

Bored and hungry, standing watch as Jenk slept, I had the catabolizer and felt as safe as I could be. We had used up the last food still in the Conn, and had plans to make another run to the small hold once Jenk awoke. Six hours later, my grumbling stomach and utter boredom got the best of me. For all I knew, Raskin could have been dead somewhere and I was sitting there starving for no reason. I left my central watch position and went to Hall 1, peering into the dim green gloom. Nothing. I did the same with Hall 3. Then, because I thought I was so clever, I popped randomly over to 2, 3, 1 and then 3 again. Nothing.

I yawned. My stomach growled. So I stepped out into 2, toward the small hold. I stopped, looking back into the Conn. Behind the console, I could hear Jenk faintly snoring. I reached for the door and it opened with a slight creak. As I began to step in, I heard an odd noise and stopped. Then there was silence again. I listened hard, willing myself to hear through the thick walls. Nothing.

Finally, I moved. Quickly, I popped the lid of a half-crate and grabbed the last two ReadiMeals, then stepped back through the door. I shut it again with as little noise as I could, and turned back to the Conn.

And saw Raskin standing over Jenk, holding that portable laser scalpel — the same one he used to kill Oleg.

I froze, the ReadiMeals thudding to the metal floor, plastic wrappers crackling as they came to rest.

We locked eyes.

I took a step forward. And he leaned closer to Jenk with the scalpel. I pulled up.

"Hello again, Peter," he said.

Sweat began to form on my brow as tension filled my body. Raskin and I looked like mirror images of each other, frozen in space. Our two weapons, the scalpel and the catabolizer, each probably had a range of less than 10 centimeters, though neither of us seemed inclined to join in that sort of close combat at the moment.

Then the catabolizer in my hand dimmed and the humming stopped. My eyes went wide as I looked down at it. With my other hand, I hit it, hoping that futile action would have some impact. Raskin leaning back, more upright, scratching his beard and smirking at me.

I did the only think I could think of.

"Jenk!" I shouted, hoping the small extra space between them was enough.

Jenk lurched awake, his body full of latent energy from our days of restless waiting now switching instantly to kinetic energy. Seeing the mad doctor above him, our nightmare come true, he flailed his hands. And the laser scalpel flew out of reach and across the floor of the Conn. Raskin jolted backward and away, as Jenk pushed at him and leaped up to stand.

Then we all regarded each other, formed into a triangle with Jenk and

Raskin on opposite sides of the Conn and me slightly down Hall 2.

And in my hand, the catabolizer hummed back to life. Suddenly three pairs of eyes were looking at my right hand. I lifted the weapon and held it toward Raskin, taking a step into the Conn.

He bolted out the door and into the darkness of Hall 1.

For a moment, Jenk and I just looked at each other. Then he spoke.

"Get after him!" he said as he turned and bent down for the scalpel on the floor. I nodded and ran over toward the door where Raskin had disappeared.

Suddenly, as I turned the corner, out of the gloom came a face, two hands, and a metal half-crate slamming into my head. Raskin only feigned running off, to get a weapon of his own. I fell hard, back into the console, losing the catabolizer.

Raskin leaped for it, grabbing the sleek humming tube. By then, Jenk had the scalpel and stepped in front to confront Raskin. I scurried backward to the wall as Raskin and Jenk circled each other in the middle of the Conn, Jenk waving the red-tipped laser scalpel and Raskin holding my humming sealant catabolizer. Like two old swashbuckling swordsmen, but with the strangest weapons you've ever seen.

I thought Jenk could take him, after all he had the command training, which included tactical skills. Raskin was *just the doctor*. Like I was *just the purser*. Jenk stepped left, then slashed right as Raskin dodged back. Raskin made a curving sweep that Jenk easily dodged, and I thought it was a matter of time before Jenk would have this under control.

Then Raskin thought of something.

"Computer. Medical Override 46-I-0. Immediate shutdown procedures," he said with an evil twinkle in his eyes.

Jenk cocked his head to one side, not knowing what this obscure reference meant. Until the laser scalpel in his hand went completely dead.

Raskin didn't wait. In the moment Jenk looked down to see the laser was off, the doctor stabbed forward, hitting Jenk in the gut with the catabolizer. Jenk screamed a hideous scream, suddenly filled with gurgling. His midsection began to *melt* in front of our very eyes, his body's molecules breaking down in the beam of the catabolizer. Raskin didn't let up, sweeping the beam across Jenk's body and watching as it tore him apart. Jenk fell in a bubbling mass of red, yellow and black goo, still alive as his body disintegrated.

The doctor then turned to look at me. And I jumped up and fled into the darkness of Hall 1.

* * *

Thinking about it now, I wonder how I had the energy. I have no energy left. Everything is so dry. I just lie on the floor of Observation. And that dot flickered again. It seemed bigger. CCC said something. Why was it so hard to listen, to pay attention? CCC started speaking again and I was straining to focus on the sound. *"...Inbound vessel..."*

I ran. He ran. Turns, green glowing lights flying by, punctuating the darkness of halls, rooms. The damn ship wasn't all that big, but I figured if he could stay hidden in it for days, I could at least try. I took off my boots in an attempt to run quietly.

My first thought was to head to Storage, but that was too obvious. I took a twisted route and ended up in Med Bay, slapping off the lights and then stepping over the remains of Artemis in the near dark. I sidled around the hulking drill suit and remains of Oleg. The smell was awful. Sweetness and rot, the metallic scent of blood clogging my nose.

I slipped in a pool of fluid, from Artemis or Oleg or Dr. Luthra, I don't know which, and slid into the back wall where a lab coat was hanging. I grabbed for it to stop my slide, but it didn't hold me and I thudded down behind the twisted gurney, the lab coat fell on top of me. The sound echoed. I froze.

In moments, he appeared at the door, holding the humming catabolizer and wearing Jenk's PCL. He scanned the room as I held my breath, ducked down low in the dark. The lab coat helped camouflage my head. Then I noticed it was one of Raskin's green coats, his name tag still pinned on. I dared not move.

He stepped forward slowly, silently, suspiciously. Over Artemis, around Oleg, closer.

I thought for sure he had seen me and was just playing coy, toying with his prey. But he moved past me to the door to Recovery.

Pausing in the doorway, he had a thought. He had taken one of the personal comm links from the Conn, and he lifted it to his mouth to speak.

I held Raskin's green lab coat over my head, then realized… I was still wearing my own PCL, and it was turned on.

Raskin tapped the control and spoke. "Where are you, Peter?" It came not only from his mouth but also echoed through my PCL. He heard it and whipped his gaze to find me. With a gasp, I jumped up and over the gurney, racing out the door.

Again through the halls, blindly changing directions, his footsteps too close behind. I threw aside the green lab coat and tore off the PCL, leaving it somewhere behind.

I did what a purser would do. I went to Storage.

Looking over my shoulder, I could see that I had put a little distance between us. Raskin wasn't in view as I reached the main door to Storage. Beside it was a console and I quickly flipped three overrides and confirmed the changes with CCC. It was a bastardized use of protocol stuff that pursers often memorized, to make our job easier. Load and unload as fast as possible.

I stepped into Storage and Raskin hit me at a dead run. That probably saved my life, since he lost control of the catabolizer and it went spinning off into some corner. I turned and slammed closed the main door, spinning the lock, then he was on me again. We wrestled across the open floor of Storage, rolling over and over. He tried to keep a hold on me, but I rolled him into the corner of a crate at an awkward angle and he winced. I took the opportunity and jumped to my feet.

Turning, I spied my one chance. The safety box. I ran.

He knew my mind too well and jumped up to run, too.

We hit the box at the same moment, cramming inside the tiny space. In the back, the large red door button was blinking, ominously. We struggled to gain position, to push the other out while staying in. But we knew that pushing the button before the door was closed would mean the death of both of us. First he was out, then he twisted and I was left hanging out into the bay. Again, we switched. Back and forth, scratching into each other's skin for a hold, pushing, pulling, twisting, stiffening.

Finally, with a quick motion, I pushed up and Raskin was slammed head first into the metal roof. He paused, stunned, and I kicked forward, sending him into the main floor of Storage, surrounded by all the crates and boxes. I pulled the hatch in one motion, twisted the closure.

Through the tiny window, he stared at me, wide-eyed. In the glass, I saw the reflection of my own bearded face superimposed over his. We looked the same. Then he pounced toward the door and I leaned back, slamming my right palm on the red door button.

Pursers move a lot of crates in Storage, in and out. When you do it enough, you get sick of waiting for the door alarm and warning countdown. So some of us take advantage of three special overrides to be able to open the main doors instantly. That's what happened.

With no warning, the back wall of Storage split and opened onto dead space. I saw Raskin give one last look of shock and fear, and then that expression was frozen on his face for all time as he was sucked out into the nothingness, along with every crate in Storage and all the air that had filled that room.

I sat in the box, catching my breath, as the dead doctor's frozen body drifted away in space. As my heart rate tried to come back to normal, I thought for a second of joining him, giving up. I was so far from home. And now I was totally alone.

Finally, I pushed the button again and the doors closed. The red light blinked for another 8 minutes as air was returned to the room. Then it went green and I opened the hatch, stepping out.

* * *

My eyes barely open. No water for days. I can't move anymore. The flickering dot was clearly a ship. RB class: technically they were Retrieval Boats, but everyone called them Rescue Buckets. Not a lot of comfort, but a ride home. It was coming. Lying still on the floor of Observation, I can see it pass among the distant stars. I think I can hold on for a few more hours, a day. CCC started speaking again. What is it saying? *"...Estimated arrival: 18 —"*

Eighteen *what?* The message repeated and I locked on to the sound, using the last of my will to pay attention to the words. *"...Estimated arrival: 18 days, 4 hours, 32 minutes."* That dot flickered like a tease. It was *right there* but the space between us was so great. The damned space between.

I'm going to close my eyes for a minute.

The Last

I awoke on the shoreline as twilight clouds rolled overhead. The waves continued their endless crashing against the smoothly-rounded black rocks of the shore. Standing like sentinels risen from the water, stone monoliths randomly broke the monotonous skyline, black against the mottled grey sky. I pushed up my visor with a hiss of released air and rolled over. A dozen meters away or so, reddish prismatic columns of basalt staggered upward into hills topped with rough grass.

Where the hell am I?

I sat up and twisted off my thick gloves. Damn, it was cold. My heavy suit kept me warm, but my exposed face and hands instantly succumbed to the chilly wind. Looking down, I saw the name — my name — JOHANNESSEN, printed on a strip affixed to the chest of my suit.

My name was Johannessen. That was a start.

I stepped toward the hills, slowly at first, then gaining momentum. As I walked, the rocks churned under my feet, hampering my progress. Still, I plodded up the hill in my heavy suit. I used the basalt columns like stepping stones, gaining ground. Soon I reached the rough grass and pulled myself toward the top of the rise. The exertion was good; it warmed me.

I thought as I walked. *Maybe my name isn't Johannessen. Maybe I found the suit. Maybe Johannessen is just whoever had it last.*

That was a strange thought. No, the suit was a perfect fit, and I knew how to open the visor and take off the gloves instinctively. My name was probably Johannessen. But it didn't sound familiar. Had I been drugged?

At the top of the hill, I turned back toward the sea. It stretched out below me and off into infinity. The jutting rocks only broke the water's surface very near the shore. Beyond them was nothing but grey clouds, grey sky, grey water.

Turning around, I looked inland. More hills. More basalt columns. More grass.

This was a world of repetition and monotony.

But, I rationalized, *I'm here. So it makes sense that* somebody else *must be here, too.* I kept walking, up and down the hills. Sound dwindled as I left the ocean behind. After several hills, an eerie silence filled the air.

In the lee of one hill, I finally saw an irregular shape. Its color was dark, nearly black, and I almost overlooked it as a shadow. But it had a straight edge. It was a roof. I changed directions, toward it, my pace increasing.

There was no movement, just a small building. Maybe a house or little barn or some place for storage. But there was nothing else nearby, so I assumed house. It seemed to be made of wood, a dark wood that had grown even darker over time. Approaching it, I saw that it was covered in a mat of dark lichens. The roof was insulated by a thick covering of moss, also very dark. On one side there was the indication of a window, but it was shuttered. Near the middle of the low building was a closed door. I stepped in front of it and knocked.

My knuckles rapped on the door's lichen-covered, damp wood, creating not the sharp, high-pitched knock I expected, but instead of series of dull thumps. No answer came. Reaching down, I clutched the knob. I didn't turn, and pushing inward had no effect. Finally, I simply pulled, and the door eased open in front of me. I stepped back to allow it to swing wide.

My knuckles tingled. I looked down and saw bits of the lichen sticking there, and absently I brushed them away, making my other hand tingle a bit, too. I looked up to study the doorway.

Though the outside was dim and grey, it stood in sharp contrast to the interior of the house. No light seemed to penetrate within, and I was left with the impression that I was looking into an abyss.

I leaned forward, but there was no improvement in visibility. I stepped in.

For several moments, I could discern nothing within. Just darkness. Keeping my back to the open door and the brighter outside world, I willed my eyes to adjust. At last I began to recognize a human form. My own shadow, dimly laid out before me. From there, I started to see other details: the floor, the edge of the wall. I took two steps farther into the room.

The room was nearly empty, just a box. But it was much smaller than the outside form, meaning there were other rooms. I saw a rectangular patch somehow darker than the other darkness: a doorway.

I realized I was holding my breath. For a moment, sparkles floated in front of my eyes, and I wondered where they came from, before finally realizing they we only in my mind. I blinked them away.

What are you afraid of, Johannessen? I asked, trying to make the name feel right. I smirked at the lunacy of it, which had the desired effect of calming me down. I entered the second room.

Johannessen. How do you even pronounce that name? Where does it come from? And more importantly, how can my own name be so alien *to me?* I looked down at the patch on my chest, barely able to see it in the darkness, and realized there was a tiny glass dome next to it. A light. I fumbled at my chest with both hands, feeling for a switch or button but finding nothing. I felt the suit at the hips, waist, down the arms. On my left forearm was some kind of flexible pad, and I pressed it inward.

Where previously the darkness was nearly complete, hiding most everything from view, now the blinding light made vision impossible. I squeezed my eyes shut forcefully.

Slowly, I allowed my face to relax, letting the light though my closed eyelids start to adjust my vision. *Any idea what else the suit can do, Johannessen?* After another moment, I opened my right eye, ever so slightly. The light was so bright it seemed to wash out all detail. But gradually I began to see.

And in the corner of the room I saw the man.

I jumped backward, bumping into something by the doorway with my head. The man didn't move or make any sound. How could he? He was only a skeleton. *Maybe he's Johannessen*, I thought, head pulsing in pain.

Reaching up to where I'd hit my head, my hand came away sticky. Something inside my head burned. *Blood. Damn.* I had nothing to wipe my hands with, but I figured the man wouldn't mind, so I wiped my blood on the wall in three vertical streaks. After, I rubbed my hands together to dry wash the rest away. The wound tingled, reminding me briefly of something, but I couldn't hold the idea in my mind. I wanted to sleep. I tried to shake off the feeling.

Something about the skeleton was compelling me forward. The way it sat, seemingly peaceful in the corner of the room, on a small, dark chair. A rough table stood against the wall, and one hand of the skeleton's rested upon it, as if he'd just sat down for a cup of tea, and then rotted away to bone.

I reached out to touch the hand. And it disappeared.

The bones of his hand fell away to dust. *How long have you been sitting here, my friend? How long?*

Sliding my hand along the arm of the skeleton, more of it disintegrated. Only wisps of the bones remained. I raised my hand into the light and saw the dark blotches of my own blood in the creases of my fingers, collecting the dust like glue. My fingertips were covered in white.

I went back outside. There seemed to be no point in staying. Once out of the house, I pressed the flexible pad again to turn off my light. And as the light went dark, so did the world around me. The whole world turned dark and only flecks of light pulsed around. *Johannessen, hold it together*. I pressed the heels of my hands to my eyes and soon the world returned.

Walking farther inland, I came to a sort of compound. Several low dark houses set together in an area that was roughly flat. Inside three of the houses were more skeletons. Each dissolved to dust at my touch.

Desperate now, I kept walking. *How many hours has it been since the shore?*

The landscape around me was dotted with the houses, now that I was able to recognize them. And the houses were dotted with skeletons.

Nothing else. No sign of trouble, no animals, food stores, not even much furniture. It wasn't making any sense. At the corner of my eyes, stars danced.

My head hurt. My hand felt strange.

There was no one around, anywhere.

I realized I was hungry. "Come now, Johannessen, what is there to eat?" I asked myself, aloud. The sound of my voice was jarring in the silent landscape.

"Hello!" I shouted, turning around. "Hello!" Hills, grass, grey sky. No reply. Not even an echo. It was like the heavy air took my words away as soon as they were voiced.

I laughed, a harsh, abrasive noise that seemed hideously out of place in this land of nothing but quiet, still death. Having nothing to eat, and finding nothing in the houses, I walked into the tall grass, hoping to find something edible growing there. Small berries grew, so I grabbed a handful. Something in the back of my mind flashed a warning. *Don't trust indigenous.* Those words sprang up, but meant nothing to me. I tried a few of the berries, biting into them to find them horribly bitter. My tongue went numb where the berry juices splashed, so I spat them out. *Safety protocol.* More words that came to my foggy mind, without reason or sense.

Then I had an idea.

I'm the last person left alive, I thought, and just thinking it made the idea burrow into my brain. Each empty house, each skeleton fading to nothing, made me believe it more firmly. *I'm the last person left alive.*

I shook my head. "Come now. Take stock: what's the situation?" I asked aloud, getting used to talking to myself to break the otherwise complete silence. "I'm in a hilly landscape populated solely by ancient skeletons. It's cold. I'm wearing some kind of suit, and my name appears to be Johannessen. I don't have any food or water. My hand is tingling. I bloodied my head. And I probably just ingested something bad." I figured Johannessen would help me reason out what to do next. "Oh, and I woke up on a shore... I woke up on a shore wearing gloves and some kind of helmet with a visor." *Some kind of helmet.*

The bitter taste wouldn't leave my mouth. I wiped at my lips with one hand, realizing the dust of the skeleton was still on my hand, now in my mouth. I tasted the dust and the metal of my own blood.

I turned back toward the rocky beach, chiding myself. *Why'd you leave the helmet there?*

Along the way, the low houses and their dead occupants called to me. *Come in. Come in.* I had visions of sitting down in one of the houses, the last person left alive, and fading into eternity with the skeletons. I realized I couldn't even imagine the skeletons as living people. In this bleak grey world, life didn't seem natural.

I'm the last person left alive, but this world is not alive.

I shook my head again. Why was I thinking such strange thoughts? It was this *place*. This place didn't invite rational thought. It gave me a burning headache. The stars that were on the edge of my vision grew.

As I crested the last hill, I looked down upon the tumultuous grey ocean. The wind blew in my face, and the constant tone of the booming waves drowned out all else. I started down the basalt column steps toward the water's edge.

"— hannessen, come —"

A *voice*.

Crackling sounds, being swept away in the wind. I searched the shoreline for the helmet. And saw it tumbling out on a receding wave.

"— ness —" was the last sound it made before sinking below the surface. *Damn. I'm the last person left alive, and now I have nothing.*

I sat down on the grey stones of the beach, folding my arms around my bent knees. The wind blew. The clouds roiled. The waves crashed. The bitter taste in my mouth faded to a tingling.

I stared out across the pointless view. I was just going to sit, like the skeletons. I was just going to sit.

Eternity passed, or maybe a moment.

I was back in the first low house, where I had hit my head. I was turning toward the wall. Where my blood had been streaked, there was nothing. There was no sign I'd ever been there. I knew I had no future. Now I had no past. I had never been. There is no Johannessen. I am not the last person left alive, because no one is alive. Not even me. The stars twinkled across my entire field of vision.

Straight out from the shore, three orbs broke through the clouds, falling, pulling clouds down and around them as the descended. Near the water's surface, they curved, stopping their fall and redirecting their momentum to come directly toward me.

Second wave, I thought, not knowing what that meant. *No. The orbs, whatever they are… They made the people into skeletons.*

I sat and waited. I was already a skeleton.

My mouth tingled. My hand tingled. My head was on fire.

The orbs came to me, perfectly round, shining and reflecting the grey world around them. The came and hovered above me.

"JOHANNESSEN."

The orbs spoke so loudly that I cowered, startled. The harsh sound hurt my head even more.

"JOHANNESSEN — STATUS?"

What?

"Who's Johannessen? Am I him?" I asked, hands rising to hold my ears.

"JOHANNESSEN — FIRST WAVE REPORT. SAFE TO LAND?"

You're asking me if it is safe? The world is full of nothing but grey and noise and silence and dust and death.

"No," I said in a low voice, dropping my eyes from the orbs back to the rocky shore.

For a moment, the orbs didn't speak. Then a section of the center orb wavered and became translucent, then clear. I was sitting inside, wearing my helmet, visor down.

"REPEAT AND CONFIRM."

"No, damn it, I said *no!*" I spat to get the tingling bitterness out of my mouth.

"GOD HELP YOU, JOHANNESSEN."

The me inside the orb disappeared and its surface became opaque again. The three shapes rose as one, then lifted straight up toward the clouds.

I fell backward on the shore, arms and legs splayed out, watching them rise directly above me, like three points of a triangle. A divine trinity of angels floating into the sky.

They disappeared into the angry clouds and the world was empty again.

Grey and dead and silent and empty.

The Vacancy of Dreams

from the world of *The Oasis of Filth*

Yoo Hyun-woo was born on the fourteenth day of April in the year 2003 to Korean immigrant parents in Milbourne, Pennsylvania. Though his parents spoke English fluently, his father had an excellent job, and their stature in society was secure, Hyun-woo's biggest fear living in America was not fitting in. Plus, he got sick of everyone mispronouncing his name. So, to his parents' dismay, he went by Hank.

He had ten years of a normal life.

In the late summer of 2013, Hank was lazily reading in bed in his room at home — an apartment in a low brick building that cornered on Market Street. As a ten year old, Hank had no consideration whatsoever for the news. It wasn't that he avoided it, it was more that he couldn't possibly have cared less what the news had to say, even when his mother sat in front of the television, entranced by some earnest live news report.

Blaring from the other room, Hank heard the television clearly, but only certain words stood out: "infected," "military," "fighting." Then, from outside his window, he heard the sound of something glass being shattered on the street. Hank jumped out of bed and looked out the window. A crowd had formed. From above, it was like the shape of a bull's eye: people in the middle surrounded by a ring of others. Hank saw a person holding a shovel, swinging it toward another person. "Mom!" he yelled. "Mom, what's going on?"

He realized the television had gone silent. His mother didn't reply. Hank swung open the door to his room and stepped into the hall, suddenly afraid. "Mom?"

At the end of the hall, there was a light. Hank walked toward it. Rounding the corner, he realized the front door to their apartment was open. His mother must've gone outside. She wouldn't have gone far, wouldn't have left him alone. She'd never done that before. "Mom?" he called out again, in a voice slightly trembling. Hank stepped out of the apartment and, following the sound of voices, one of which he thought might be his mother, he went down the stairs to the ground floor.

The main door to the building was also open. The light outside was bright, the interior dark. The contrast made it hard to focus on what was outside, but he could tell by the noise there were people. "Mom?" Outside, someone shrieked and a great commotion started up. People were running, some past him and up the stairs. "Mom!" he called out frantically. Hank heard popping sounds, and thought someone, maybe one of the bully teenagers that lived nearby, must've been lighting off firecrackers.

There was another scream, and another. More popping. Hank couldn't comprehend why there was so much trouble about silly fireworks. As a woman ran in the door way, frantic, he hugged the doorframe and poked his head out into the sunlight.

Several loud pops happened on his left, and he turned in time to see two people fall to the ground.

There was blood.

Hank whipped his head around, searching. "Mom!" Then he saw her, running toward him. His mother had a terrible expression on her face, one he would never forget. She had always been there for him, reliable, steady, strong. But she was scared. No, she was terrified. He noticed tears streaking down her cheeks. She called out his name. More pops sounded. Other people streamed left and right between them, blocking his view. When they cleared, Hank's mother was gone.

No, not gone. She was on the ground.

She wasn't moving.

"*Mom!*" Hank shouted, in a shrill, frightened voice. Heedless of any other concern, he ran out into the street toward her. Before he had taken ten steps, his father appeared, diving down toward the still form of his mother. His father was also crying, trying to pick up his mother. The street below her was red and wet. In a low voice, Hank said, "Dad? How'd you get here?" Hank stood, frozen, confused.

His father turned, still holding the crumpled form of his mother, and looked at Hank. Hank had never seen his father face the way it looked then. His father was always composed, always sure. Now, his face was twisted with grief, anger, fear, dismay. Without another glance down, his father lowered the body — for that's all it seemed to be anymore — of his mother, and he stood. He turned away from Hank, and Hank swiveled his head to see what his father was looking at.

Men.

Men in green, with guns. Walking in some sort of formation.

Hank's father stepped over his mother lying in the street and ran toward the nearest one of them, yelling a terrible, guttural sound like a raging monster, his fists balled and high in the air.

Hank knew what would happen before it did. "Dad!" he yelled. "No!"

The man in green, the one his father was racing toward, turned and aimed his gun. *Pop.*

His father fell. *Pop.* A second, for good measure.

The man in green, the soldier, turned without another concern and continued walking in formation with the others.

Hank fell to his knees in disbelief. He was no longer scared. He was no longer concerned by the mob around him, the noise, the danger. He no longer cared. He only cried. He was only grief and nothing more.

* * *

Hank held his palms against his eyes, trying to block out the bright lights. It was loud, people moving everywhere, but he sat on the hard plastic seat. Absently, he assumed he was waiting. For what, he had no idea.

"Do you want to see the doctor?" a voice asked.

Hank blinked, slowly, and looked up. "What?"

"Do you want to see the doctor?" the voice repeated. But there was a commotion.

Another voice called out. "Hyun-woo!" Hank cringed.

"Dad?" he called sheepishly. *How could Dad be here*, he thought, *after what I saw?* But the voice. It sounded like his father.

A face appeared before him, blurry in the blinding light, blurry from the tears. Hank blinked once, twice. Finally, recognition. "Uncle Manny?" he asked, unsure.

"Come on, boy, let's get out of here." An arm went around his shoulder, comforting but urging. Hank got up and followed. Out in the bright sunlight. Shading his eyes, he saw the tank rolling down the street. The streets of his city. A place he no longer knew.

* * *

Hank's uncle Min-woo Yoo — he ordered his name in the American way — was Army Corps of Engineers, and everyone in the Army called him Manny. It stuck. Virtually no one called him anything else. Being in the service apparently had given Uncle Manny enough access, enough warning, to locate his nephew before it was too late. Before Hank was shipped off to some 'destination.'

Months passed as Hank lived like a ghost in the apartment with his uncle and his Aunt Ji-yeon, doing whatever was asked of him — and only that — like he walked through the scenes of a movie, reality gone dull around the edges. Hank learned of a disease that was spreading, something they were calling RL2013, and how it was turning normal people into raging monsters. In the streets and at school, people called the diseased people 'zombies.'

Hank tried to remember. *Were there zombies that day?* But then visions of his mother, his father, would swell up, and Hank would squeeze his eyes trying to make the pictures in his mind go away.

When Uncle Manny announced one day that they had to leave, to pull within the fortifications of Philadelphia, Hank welcomed the chance to leave Milbourne for good.

Jangling keys the next day, Aunt Ji-yeon asked him to accompany her on one last visit to his parent's apartment — his *home* — and as she shuffled around, collecting things she deemed important, Hank saw a letter lying open on the table by the television. *Surely*, he thought, *it must've been read by Mom. Just before...* He squeezed his eyes shut again for a moment. Carefully, Hank lifted the paper.

And he discovered Fullerton, California.

* * *

Peace, joy, tranquility, family, freedom. Hank read the letter over and over, from his mother's cousin, a woman Hank had never met, or at least couldn't remember. Fullerton took up residence in Hank's brain. It was everything his life was not; an icon he could not forget.

Moving inside the walls of Philadelphia, they were forced to live in small, sterile apartments. Cleanliness was not merely requested, it was required. 'Stay clean, stay alive,' was the mantra Hank was forced to memorize. He was enrolled in a bloated, overpopulated school, a place where cleanliness became a full-time job for not only the custodial staff — who seemed to be everywhere all the time — but also for each administrator and teacher. And it became an especially important job for the students. Cleanliness was a primary factor in being promoted in grade, getting better class assignments, and avoiding trouble. At least with the teachers. Quite the opposite was true once school was dismissed. Hank was no stranger to bullies; the only change was who they bullied and why.

For Hank, bullies loved to pick on him because he was clean, and clean meant he was one of teacher's favorites. The bullies would push him down, force him to get dirty. Hank spent many evenings diligently scrubbing his school clothes. It gave him time to fall into his thoughts again, wall himself up inside his anguish.

The grief that held an iron grip on Hank's heart since the death of his parents grew deeper and more profound, to the unavoidable feeling that there was simply no point in living. The only thing that sparked his mind was Fullerton. He reread the letter often, before going to sleep at night. The apartment was too small for him to have his own room, so he was forced to sleep on the couch. It was a place without privacy, but nonetheless, he tucked the letter and a few other personal things behind the couch for safekeeping, in a little sack he kept. He knew it was pointless. Aunt Ji-yeon certainly recognized the things were there, as she cleaned meticulously on a daily basis.

Hank harbored an anger toward his uncle and aunt for what his life had become, and yet he also felt guilt, knowing that it wasn't their fault. He strongly suspected they had their own resentment for having to suddenly welcome a child into their lives. But in time, the mutual sense of family and obligation between them did become a sort of love. While Aunt Ji-yeon expressed her love more passively, Uncle Manny liked taking Hank places.

As an engineer with the Army, Uncle Manny got to travel a lot more than most people. He had his own jeep, and was in charge of the management of an entire section of the southern wall. Some mornings, he would

awaken Hank, saying, "Nephew. Do you want to come with me today?"
Hank always said yes.

Strictly speaking, there wasn't a rule saying that Hank couldn't tag
along, but everyone knew it would be bad for the city officials to find
out, and could easily result in disciplinary action against Manny. For this
reason, no one they ever encountered — the crews Uncle Manny
supervised, colleagues, and other engineers — ever said a word. The
higher ranking folks might tousle Hank's hair, but rarely would they
speak to him. Those in lower ranks would smile and call out to him.
Having a kid around felt kind of normal. They liked it.

* * *

Years passed. When Hank turned 14, he had grown significantly, though
he still had the rounded, fresh look of a kid, especially compared to his
uncle.

Uncle Manny still enjoyed taking Hank with him to work, when possible,
and so it was on one particular Saturday morning that Hank stepped out
of his uncle's jeep and saw something he never expected. Something that
would change his life forever.

A girl.

Her name was Janine Francis and she was a year younger. A bit of a
tomboy despite her long, braided hair, Janine was a tag-along herself.
Her father, a colleague of Uncle Manny's, had seen Hank so many times
that he finally decided to chance it and bring his daughter to work. The
crews were silent, surprised to see the young new face, particularly
female. But no one was more surprised than Hank. He tried to recall if he
had seen this girl at school, but he didn't think so. Didn't think it was
possible for that to have happened and he didn't remember. Because
Hank immediately thought to himself, *she's beautiful.*

The word 'beautiful' was not something Hank thought about or ever used
in conversation. So when he realized it was precisely the word he was
thinking, he was taken aback. He stared at Janine with his mouth agape,
as she approached. Slightly unsure of herself for being there, Janine

looked away. But despite the nervousness, the newness, the obviousness of his stare, Janine couldn't help herself. She had to comment.

In a low voice as she walked by, Janine looked up at Hank, batting eyes that he suddenly found himself swimming in, and said, "You tryin' to catch flies or something?"

Hank's complexion turned three or four shades redder as he clamped his mouth closed.

* * *

It was weeks before he saw her again, though he went with Uncle Manny to work whenever he could, hoping for a chance encounter. The anticipation was like an alien life form invading his body; it was the first set of feelings he'd had since his parents died that weren't tinged with anger, fear, sadness, or hopelessness. With all the subtlety his teenage mind could conjure, he discovered her name simply by asking his uncle, who in turn asked the girl's father. It was embarrassing but efficient. Subsequently, Hank had to admit to himself that if he saw her again, she'd already know he was interested.

When their paths next intersected, on another random day of tagging along, it was Janine who broke the ice. "Have you ever looked over the wall?" she asked him as the adults talked shop.

Hank was almost too shy to respond. With a tiny shake of his head, he reminded himself to play it cool, to attempt to act normal. "No," was all he said, curtly. Inside, he cursed himself for coming off so rude.

Janine seemed unaffected. "Well, I'm going to climb up and have a look." She paused a moment, then said, "You coming?" With an expression that was part disbelief, part terror, and part elation, Hank nodded and chased after her.

* * *

They spent a good part of that morning just sitting on the wall, high above the lost world. After that, Hank continuously pestered his uncle to include him on work days, and Janine began to do the same with her father. Crews working around the fortifications became very familiar with the two teens wandering together along the fringes of the wall, or sitting at the top. They received countless knowing smiles from the men working, but no one said a thing. In a world of stifling control, danger, and disease, young love was a joy for everyone to witness.

For their part, Hank and Janine did what teenagers do when given time and privacy. They talked a lot, about nothing at first, but later growing into more profound topics. The world they lived in was not a place of dreams, and yet they each found themselves dreaming a little when they were together. Hank's genuine happiness, he thought, was like the turning of seasons. He had experienced the long march to winter but now a new spring had appeared before him.

Eventually, a topic came up that changed things. It was a warm day as they sat atop the wall, looking over the alien outside world, full of roads and buildings, but no people. The wall had only been in place for a few years, and was continually expanded upon and improved. From their viewpoint, the world outside the wall seemed nearly the same as before, though the grass grew long and some things lay broken and unattended. But mostly the world seemed fine. Seeing it so helped with their escapism, made them feel even more connected, both to each other as well as the world beyond.

Slowly, carefully, Janine spoke. "What happened to your parents?" Hank turned away, not able to conceal his surprise and sorrow at the sudden memories. She put a hand on his shoulder and waited. There was no point asking again. He would tell or he wouldn't; it would change things between them, or it wouldn't.

After a moment, he turned back, wearing an expression she had never seen on his face, squinty and tormented, near tears. Still he paused, and when he spoke, he almost sounded normal. "Dead. Shot by the military. I guess they thought they were infected or something. Nothing else makes sense. Both of them, in just a few minutes. Right in front of our apartment. Right in front of me." As Hank looked down at his empty, upturned palms, Janine simply hugged him and that was all.

* * *

Their discussions gained depth as they spent more time together. They began to share their teenage angst, Hank's being mostly grief over his parents, while Janine had an uncontrollable fear of the future. Of course, they shared frustrated stories of adults in control, school, bullies, and demands on their time they didn't understand. But Janine's greater fear was *What's next?* What terrible thing was next to befall them and the world they lived in? Could the disease get them? Could they really prevent it? What happened when they grew up, even if they lived? Would they waste their lives in some hideously dull assigned job? What choice did they have about anything? "These walls," Janine told Hank one day in a sullen voice, thumping the solid metal wall with her fist, "aren't to keep the bad people out. They're to keep us in this prison."

As she spoke, Hank scanned the seemingly normal world outside the wall. "I know a place. Out there." He gestured one hand toward the setting sun.

"The Oasis?" Janine asked, looking at him sidelong.

"Maybe."

"No one knows where it is," she said. "Or at least not for sure."

"I have an idea."

"Where?" she asked, leaning closer.

Hank squinted into the descending red ball of the sun. "California."

* * *

One morning in the fifteenth year of Hank's life, Uncle Manny stepped lightly to where Hank slept on the couch and gently shook him awake, a process he had done so many times before. Hank was getting larger with each passing year, and as he stood, stretching, Uncle Manny realized they were now the same height. "Nephew, I want you to see something new. Come with me." In short order, Hank was in the passenger seat of Uncle Manny's jeep as they drove along, but not to the usual location.

Someplace new, a little farther away.

They turned into a well-concealed alley that ran along the wall, a place where the fortifications were doubled, one on each side of the little road. The path led to a dead end. As the jeep rolled to a stop in front of the squared off section of wall, Uncle Manny killed the engine and stepped out. "What is this place?" Hank asked, still tired and yawning.

Uncle Manny walked forward to the wall and placed one hand on its flat surface, near a vertical seam. "Hank, listen carefully. I'm not supposed to bring you here, but you're old enough now that I want you to know… in case."

"In case what?"

His uncle came up and gently took Hank by the shoulders so they could look eye to eye. "You should know, more than most, Hank. *Bad things can happen*." Uncle Manny dropped his grip on Hank's shoulders and continued. "I don't know anything for sure, but I can see something's wrong. I'm worried bad things are about to happen *here*, in the city. A lot of people I know feel the same."

Hank was silent. He knew his own version of bad things, but couldn't quite grasp what his uncle was telling him. "But," he asked with a curious tilt of his head, "what does that have to do with this?" He nodded toward the dead end wall in front of them.

"I'll show you." Uncle Manny stepped back to the wall, placing his hand flat again near the same vertical seam. "This," he said, almost like an announcement, "is where you go if you need to get out." And then he pushed.

The solid wall pivoted away smoothly, like the opening of a door. Hank's mouth fell open in amazement. Seconds before he would have sworn the wall to be solid and impenetrable. Now, with one hand, his uncle had opened a gate large enough for the jeep to get through. Beyond, Hank could see the interior of the wall, a width of 30 feet, and another flat section of wall cutting off the way on the other side. "But…" he started.

"The other side works the same way, Hank. Push, and it opens."

"Isn't that… unsafe? Won't the zombies get in?" Hank said, taking a step backward in sudden alarm.

Uncle Manny shook his head and gave a slight chuckle. "Don't forget, we're engineers. This thing is like a valve. Push from this side and it opens. Push from the other side and it won't budge. And that's important. If you use it, it's one way only."

"But…" he said again. His uncle waited. "But *why*?"

"Contingencies, nephew. Contingencies. What does the wall do, Hank?"

"It keeps the zombies out," he replied.

"Correct, but what *else* does it do?" Uncle Manny probed.

Thinking back to what Janine said, he knew the answer at once. "It keeps us in."

Uncle Manny smiled a rich smile, slowly nodding. "Absolutely right. And what do you do if you *have to get out*?"

"I could come here?" It was more question than statement.

"Absolutely right."

* * *

At school, things continued along their expected course, the teachers, administrators, and even the bullies acting their parts, like today was the same as yesterday, as every day. But one thing seemed different. At first, Hank didn't recognize what had changed. After lunch, he asked the teacher if he could leave class briefly to use the bathroom. Of course, the bullies sneered. *Teacher's pet has privileges, assholes*, he thought. As he left the classroom, he walked down an empty hall, lost in thought. Turning left by rote, he put one hand out to open the bathroom door and it swung away from him, like… Like what? He paused. *Like the valve. In the wall.* Hank looked up, turning his head to scan down the hall in both directions.

Where are the custodians? he thought.

* * *

Back at home, Hank noticed that people were getting restless. Neighbors who usually kept to themselves were out in the streets, talking, sometimes shouting. Things felt *tense*.

In many ways, Hank remained a self-absorbed teenager. His biggest concern, through the changes and commotion, wasn't worrying about what the adults were doing. He was worried about his 16th birthday.

But not for himself, not specifically. Not to get presents lavished upon him. It was for a simpler reason: Janine had told him to make sure to meet her at the wall fortifications compound on his birthday. "Promise me you'll be here. You *have* to get your uncle to bring you that day," she had told him with a deep sincerity.

"I promise."

But in the days leading up to his birthday, Hank rarely saw his uncle. Uncle Manny was too busy, too many things were going on. Hank became frantic that he would miss this special day, ruin whatever Janine had planned, or more importantly, miss seeing her. He waited up one evening, despite Aunt Ji-yeon's protests, for his uncle to come in very late from work.

Finally, the door lock clicked and Uncle Manny stepped in quietly, expecting the apartment to be asleep. He hung his coat and hardhat, slipped off his shoes, and padded lightly into the living room. There, he inhaled quickly, a little surprised to find Hank under a dim light, waiting for him. Quietly, he asked, "What're you doing up still, nephew?"

"Uncle Manny, I need a favor," Hank replied, then fell silent. His chin dipped toward his chest, half in exhaustion but half in fear of rejection.

His uncle came and sat next to him on the couch. "Well, I'll have to hear what it is before I can say yes or no."

"I need to go to work with you on my birthday. To the wall."

Uncle Manny scratched absently at the stubble on his cheeks, flecks of black and silver, from the long day. "Well. You know I would be happy to take you. But, recently, my work has changed quite a bit. I don't know if I'll be going to the wall that day. I—"

"But I really *need* to be there then!" Hank almost shouted, interrupting his uncle.

Uncle Manny's eyes went wide and he slowly leaned away, surprised by Hank's urgency. His fingers stopped scratching his cheek, and he dropped his hand to his lap. "Something going on?"

"No. Yes. Well, I think so. Maybe," Hank stammered.

Uncle Manny paused a moment and nodded. "Is this about your friend? Janine?" Hank nodded and Uncle Manny just sat, noting again how Hank had grown, how he wasn't only tall but had put on bulk. Hank was nearly a man. "Nephew, I know she means a lot to you. I'll do what I can."

* * *

Uncle Manny kept his word. By the day of his 16th birthday, Hank stood slightly taller than his uncle, weighing nearly the same. Though his uncle was not fat, Hank's weight was almost exclusively muscle. The benefits of youth. Together that morning, the man and the nearly-man stepped up into the jeep and headed for the wall. Uncle Manny couldn't help but be proud and harbor a smile. This person was not his son, not by birth, but in every other way, that was how he thought of Hank. Hank was his son.

A boy of 10, who had grown into a 16-year-old verging on manhood, was going to meet his love. Uncle Manny knew a spade was a spade. He knew Hank and Janine were in love, and he thought it was like cool breeze in the dead of summer: an unexpected, and lovely, relief. Since Hank was 10, Uncle Manny wondered what would become of him, where he would go. Unlike Hank's real parents, it was easier for Uncle Manny to envision a world *without* Hank. Not because he didn't love the boy. He did. At first, it was more or less duty and family, but over the years, he had come to legitimately love Hank. He would do nearly anything for him. Such as skip out on his work schedule to shuttle Hank to a date.

As they pulled up and stepped out of the jeep, Hank was all nerves. Uncle Manny simply watched from the driver's seat of the jeep as Hank walked off toward the wall, unable to hide his head sliding side to side searching for Janine.

But they both could see. She wasn't there.

"If she said she'll be here, give her time, nephew. She'll be along," Uncle Manny said calmly.

It was another 43 minutes before Janine arrived.

Janine's father drove into the work lot faster than normal, skidding to a stop in the gravel. Instantly, the passenger door popped open and Janine jumped out, hiding her face with one hand and running off toward the wall. She brushed passed Hank and he turned and followed her. As Janine found a corner where they wouldn't be seen, she turned and buried her face against Hank's chest, shaking. He realized she was crying. "What is it?" he asked, a feeling of dread turning into a ball of stone in his stomach.

At first she wouldn't talk, then finally, with his prompting, Janine looked up, tears sliding down paths on her cheeks. "My father…" She looked down, unable to speak the words while still looking him in the eye. "He's taking us away."

Hank was confused. The words didn't even make sense. *Taking us away?* Where was there to go? They lived in a walled city. "Wait, what?" was all he could say.

"My dad says things are going to get really bad here. He wants to take us away. To Canada. Tomorrow."

Hank's mind reeled. Janine was going to Canada? It wasn't possible. "Don't go," he said.

"I have to go. My dad says so. I tried everything. I... I..." She began crying again, and Hank pulled her closer.

"What's in Canada?" Hank asked. Already, he felt the hole inside him, the gap left by his parents, growing larger.

"Dad thinks The Oasis is there."

"But," Hank started, shaking his head, "that's... impossible."

"I told him what you think. About California."

"You did?" Hank was shocked to have this secret revealed.

"I didn't tell him it was your idea," Janine said, slightly offended at the implication. They were silent for a while, allowing the situation to come to rest within their minds while they continued to hold each other close. Finally, Janine pushed away gently and looked Hank in the eyes. "Will I ever see you again?"

He looked into her eyes, the ones he found himself swimming in. How could he be losing her? He had already lost so much. It just wasn't fair. Involuntarily, Hank's shoulders tensed and his arms tightened. His jaw clenched in anger, and despair. Still, he looked at her with a steady gaze, trying to reassure her. "Of course." Immediately, he hated himself for lying to her. He was never going to see Janine again. The thought was even worse than losing his parents. Hank was old enough to realize why. His parents gave him his life, but his life was his own. Janine was the one he wanted to share it with. If she was gone, what was there left for him in this hellish, stifling world?

They stayed together as long as they could, but eventually Janine's father called for her. Hank's heart tore apart as Janine stood on tiptoes and kissed him. "I love you. Goodbye." She turned and ran back to the waiting car.

As it pulled out of view, Hank set his jaw, teeth clenched together. He didn't shed another tear. He just watched every detail. The car, the road, the dust kicked up. When the last mote of dust touched the ground, as if

Janine had never been there, never existed, Hank blinked, only once, and made his final transition from boy to man.

* * *

For weeks, Hank returned to the work site with his uncle, hoping Janine would one day show. She never did. When two months had passed, he lost hope. In six months' time, he finally believed it was true. She was gone.

After his parents died, after he had been whisked away to this city, Hank's life was shallow. Now, even that small depth was gone and his life felt flat. There was no purpose, and no dimension. He could tell things around him weren't normal, that tensions were building. But it didn't matter to him. He simply couldn't care for the state of the world when the state of his soul was so empty.

He passed the days, so many days, for so little reason. Finally, he gave up asking to go to work with Uncle Hank, and wouldn't go along even when asked. He spent every spare moment in the apartment, barely moving. The better part of a year went by, and Hank still felt torn apart by Janine's absence.

On his last day in Philadelphia, Uncle Manny was off somewhere at work. Lost in thought, Hank hardly noticed the explosion, the shouts, the running footsteps. His aunt came to him full of worry. "Hank. Something's going on." He saw in her expression that she was scared.

"What is it, Aunt Ji-yeon?" Hank asked.

"Your uncle has been warning me. Things in the city look bad. They're not safe. But, listen. Something's going on outside." They went to the window, where they could see people running in all directions. Hank couldn't help but think of the day his parents died, the commotion outside his apartment then. Through the crowd, they saw Uncle Manny pull up quickly in the jeep. In a moment, three people were on the vehicle, clawing at it like animals. With no doors or roof, the jeep provided little protection, and Uncle Manny kicked at the people to push them back. Aunt Ji-yeon let out a shocked yelp. *Are those... zombies?*

Hank thought, incredulous.

"What're they do—" Hank began, when Aunt Ji-yeon suddenly ran out of the apartment. Hank gasped. *This can't be happening again.* He raced after her, determined not to let her out of his sight. Somehow he would keep her safe.

He chased her around and around the descending flights until she stopped quickly near the ground floor. Hank rounded the last turn and could see, over her shoulder, what was happening. A woman was lying, injured and bloody, on the floor by the door to the first apartment. Hank recognized her — Mrs. Ewing. She was bleeding out just inches from her own front door. Two other figures stood nearby. One was blocking the main entrance and the other stood at the base of the stairs, back toward Hank and Aunt Ji-yeon. Hank didn't recognize either of the men. Didn't understand when they moved closer to Mrs. Ewing, or her abject terror, her eyes bugging out.

Mrs. Ewing raised a small gun with one trembling hand and fired.

Everything happened too fast. Hank couldn't react, couldn't even comprehend. The man at the base of the stairs crumpled to the floor, and at the same moment, Aunt Ji-yeon fell, tumbling down the last flight to come to rest leaning against the strange man. "No!" Hank shouted, leaping down the stairs. He grabbed his aunt, lifting her at an angle off the floor. Her neck was covered in blood, with more gushing out. She tried to speak, but only a wet gurgle came.

Somewhere around them more shots were fired. The second man fell upon Mrs. Ewing and she screamed. There were horrible sounds, tearing sounds. Another shot. Then stillness in the corner.

Hank watched as Aunt Ji-yeon went still as well.

His vision blurred and he blinked at the tears. Finally, he saw the man lying next to them clearly. He looked savage, distorted. His teeth were bared in an awful rictus smile, his skin thick and irregular. *A zombie. Oh my God, a zombie right here.* Hank kicked at the monster, pushing it away from his aunt's body.

A figure appeared in the doorway and Hank looked up. "Uncle Manny…," he began, then looked down at his aunt's lifeless body in his arms. "She… she got shot." Uncle Manny fell to his knees, hard, then tumbled into his wife, sobbing.

They sat that way for what seemed like forever.

* * *

"Get your things. Everything you'll need," Uncle Manny said when they entered the apartment.

"Everything I'll need for what?" Hank asked.

"For life. You're leaving."

"Wait — *I'm* leaving? What about you?"

Uncle Manny didn't respond to the question. "Just get your things, nephew. Please." He turned away, heading toward the kitchen.

"No."

Uncle Manny turned back. His expression was not surprise. He knew Hank was his own man now. "Please, Hank. You need to leave."

"Not without you."

Uncle Manny huffed. "You don't need this old man tagging along when you go."

"Then I won't go."

Hank's uncle looked at the floor for a long moment before speaking. "I *can't leave her here*, nephew. I can't."

"She isn't here anymore. I'm sorry, but she's not." Hank went to his uncle. He was taller, bigger, but in the end, Hank was still the child. His uncle had taken him in and raised him. He hugged Uncle Manny, and after a moment, Uncle Manny hugged him back. "I'll leave, but you're coming with me."

Finally, Uncle Manny nodded.

* * *

They packed the jeep with food, water, some clothes, shoes. Aunt Ji-yeon's body was carefully laid in the back. At last, Uncle Manny brought out a small case, asking Hank to come near. "I've never shown this to you before, because there was never a good reason. Now there is." He opened the case to reveal a pistol and a box of ammunition. Hank nodded. Uncle Manny removed the pistol, loaded it full, then placed it in the glovebox. "Let's go."

As Uncle Manny drove the streets toward the wall, Hank noticed how different things had become. Thankfully very few people had vehicles, so they were able to avoid the angry mobs that gathered here and there. They saw several more infected, and one even leaped toward the jeep before Uncle Manny swerved to avoid it. Several times, Hank turned to look at Aunt Ji-yeon lying in the back. Afterward, he wished he hadn't.

When they arrived at the hidden valve in the wall, Uncle Manny only slowed, never stopped. The jeep pushed open the first valve and Hank felt his life changing again, telling him he would never be the same. *No, that's not right. My life has been nothing* but *changes. This is no different*. They pushed through the second valve and drove into the outside world. Taking a bridge, they entered New Jersey and turned south.

They never saw the city again, not that the city had much left anyway. Within four weeks, Philadelphia fell.

* * *

Uncle Manny drove aimlessly at first, scanning around with his eyes. Hank wasn't sure what he was looking for, until finally the jeep diverted from the road and drove through a wooded area. Uncle Manny kept scanning until he found something he liked. Without a word, he stopped the jeep on a grassy hill overlooking a wide river. Hank watched as his uncle stepped out, gingerly lifted his dead wife from the vehicle and carried her across the hillside. Finding just the spot, Uncle Manny carefully placed Aunt Ji-yeon amid the flowers. "Nephew. I'm going to need some time. She was my wife for more than 22 years. If you want to say any last words, go ahead now. But then, please let me have a moment with her." Hank nodded.

He couldn't think of anything much to say, but he sat down next to his aunt on the ground. Hank took her hand in both of his. "Aunt Ji-yeon, thank you for everything you ever did for me. You and Uncle Manny rescued me when I didn't think I could be rescued. I love you." Hank sat a few moments more and then, out of respect, walked back and sat in the jeep to leave his uncle and aunt in peace for one last time.

* * *

When Uncle Manny finally came back to the jeep, his eyes were red and raw. With an effort, he turned to look at Hank. "Where should we go, nephew?" Hank was taken aback by the question. He always expected his elders to have all the answers. Yet now he knew. His mother and father didn't know everything, couldn't. His Aunt Ji-yeon hadn't known everything, nor could Uncle Manny. Looking at the empty shell that was his uncle, he had no one but himself to rely upon. "California, I think," he said, remembering that letter, the one he had read and reread so many times. Uncle Manny looked up, eyebrows raised. "I believe The Oasis is in Fullerton, California." Whether his uncle agreed or simply moved in order to do something, anything at all, Uncle Manny started the jeep and began driving.

* * *

They were lucky for a time, finding open pathways as they followed the highway south and west, skirting Wilmington and heading toward Baltimore. Curving around the upper part of the Baltimore beltway, they finally turned truly west on route 70. Rarely did they see another human, and of those they saw, at least half were infected. The others shunned the road as they approached.

"Soon, nephew, we will need to teach you how to drive," Uncle Manny said, patting the steering wheel. Hank looked out the open passenger door at the countryside sliding by. Despite the situation, he allowed himself a little smile. He had always wanted to drive the jeep.

Somewhere west of Baltimore, their luck changed. As the jeep crested a hill and entered a long, curved dip in the road, they saw her. A woman, standing alone beside the road, walking west with her back toward them. Hearing the engine, the woman turned slightly and they realized she was carrying something in a bundle.

A baby. She has a baby.

"Uncle…" Hank began.

Uncle Manny nodded. "I see." They pulled up beside her slowly and she stopped and turned toward them. "Do you need help?" Uncle Manny asked the strange woman with the baby in her arms. Her eyes darted left and right, and suddenly Hank realized they were surrounded. Men stood on all sides. *She tricked us*, Hank thought, angrily. One, directly in front held a shotgun pointed at them.

"Turn the jeep off and get out," the man with the gun said in a loud voice. "We don't want anyone to get hurt, but I'm gonna need you to turn the jeep off and get out."

"Do as he says, nephew," Uncle Manny said, killing the engine, but Hank saw his uncle's quick look toward the glovebox. They both stepped out of the car, and Uncle Manny rounded the vehicle to stand protectively by his nephew on the passenger side. The image was somewhat comical, given Hank's height and scale, and Hank wrinkled his forehead considering it. "What is it you want? Who are you?" Uncle Manny asked the man who spoke.

"Charlie Tanger's my name," the man said, still not lowering the shotgun. Around him, more and more people appeared out of the woods: men, women, children. Everyone's eyes were on Uncle Manny and Hank, and the jeep. "You?"

"I'm Manny. This is Hank. We'd like to be on our way now."

"Listen, Manny, I won't lie to you. We want your jeep, and your supplies. But we don't want to hurt you. In fact, we think there's strength in numbers. Why don't you join us? We're headed south to The Oasis."

Unannounced, Hank spoke. "We're *going* to The Oasis. In *California*." The man named Charlie Tanger chuckled.

"It's not there."

"How would you know?" Hank asked, offended.

"I've been just about everywhere over the past few years, kid. California, Oregon, Minnesota, Ottawa. Nothing left in any of those places. It's gotta be down south." More faces popped into view. The group must've been nearly twenty people.

"And if we choose not to join you?" Uncle Manny asked. Tanger simply shrugged, the barrel point of his shotgun making his point. Hank's uncle scanned the surrounding faces and he made a decision. In a voice only Hank could hear, he said, "Get down." Then Uncle Manny got back in the jeep. On the passenger side.

"Old man, get *out* of the jeep. Don't get yourself in —" Tanger went quiet suddenly, seeing what Uncle Manny now held. The loaded pistol from the glovebox.

Hank's uncle stepped out of the jeep again and began walking around toward the driver's side. "While I appreciate your *offer*, my nephew and I will be going now." Hank watched Uncle Manny round the front of the jeep, pistol and eyes focused on Tanger.

Hank scanned the faces surrounding them. And suddenly his heart leaped into this throat, seeing a young woman step out of the forest beside the road. "*Janine*?" When she heard her name, he saw her expression turn to shock and disbelief, then a smile broke across her face. It really was her. Janine was here. Unexpectedly, the girl he thought he had lost forever had returned. Hank turned, smiling, toward his uncle, about to say that joining this group seemed like a very good idea after all.

Neither Uncle Manny nor Hank ever saw the woman with the baby pull a pistol from under the swaddling clothes until it was too late. She fired. The baby began to wail, startled by the sound.

Uncle Manny fell face first onto the highway, the gun flying from his hand.

"No!" Hank shouted.

"No!" Janine echoed, rushing forward.

They met again, young lovers reunited, this time hovering over the dying form of a man lying in the road.

The woman with the baby dropped her gun loudly to the street, then covered her face with her hand.

As he had done for his mother, his aunt, now Hank found himself clutching his dying uncle, the man who became his father when his father was gone. And a rage took him, and he became blind to all around him. Even the return of Janine was like static in a transmission, present but unable to overtake the primary signals of his brain. Like his true father before him, he turned toward revenge. Hank reached out for Uncle Manny's gun. He could feel the tension of those around him, sense the deadly barrel of Tanger's shotgun pointing at him.

And a hand stopped him. Not the strongest hand, but strong enough. A touch he hadn't felt in too long. Janine pressed herself against him. "Don't. Don't," was all she said. "Please." Slowly, the spell of anger broke and he turned toward her face. "We have each other. We've lost everyone else, but we have each other."

"Your father…?" Hank began.

Janine just shook her head, her long braids flopping across her shoulders. "There's only you. And me. Don't make me lose you again." Hank dipped his head to his chest, tears dropping onto his uncle's shirt.

Despite the pain and loss, despite the hell they lived in, despite the anguish of Uncle Manny dying right in front of him, Hank had to make a choice. To stand and fight against all odds, for those who were already gone. Or to sit and choose to do what was right for *her* and for *him*, to try to find a life for the two of them.

As Uncle Manny let out his last breath, Hank slowly nodded.

Black Fire

Of all the mages, Huldrych is, by far, the least respected. For he is the only mage — that is, the only fully grown and fully trained individual — incapable of producing black fire.

Despite years of his attempts to change, despite kind-hearted as well as not-so-kind-hearted teasing, Huldrych's flame runs white when he combines all his color fire. This is not the least bit true of any other living or (known) dead mage. Their color fires become black. It is the way things are and the way they have always been.

Huldrych is an anomaly. Or, if you listen to some of the less refined sentiments of the citizenry, a freak.

Mages live across the land, indeed throughout the entirety of the Known World. But Atys is where they mostly congregate. Atys is the capital city of mages, and therefore quite an important place.

From time to time, some outside force — and no one is truly sure where they come from, not even the wise mages — will come to invade or attack Atys, thinking it rich and ripe for the taking. Of the former note, these attackers are invariably correct; Atys is indeed quite the wealthy city. Of the latter, however, they are dead wrong. Black fire springs forth from one (or, Deus forbid, several) of the mages at their will and destroys any and all living things that dare threaten their fine city.

Until…

* * *

Mages are humans. They need to breathe, eat, sleep. They age and can be killed, just as any other human. They are like anyone else in every respect except for one: they can produce color fire. Some children exhibit the ability on their own and are immediately taken in for training. But if they make it to age four without any sign of ability, all of the children in the Known World are permitted to take The Test. It's a cruel but remarkably effective test.

To determine if a child has the gift of color fire, they are held underwater until they drown.

Though this might seem like an excellent way to rid the world of children, the mortality rate of The Test is, in actuality, slightly less than 20%. And still, parents willingly subject their children to The Test every year without fail, with extraordinarily few exceptions. Why? Because the ones who pass become apprentices, and apprentices become mages. Mages rule the Known World as a very secretive, very close knit society, albeit a competitive and ruthless one at times, too. Having a child become a mage is the most certain way for a family to improve its station and respectability. Families that produce mages over several generations gain more and more power and influence, and while they will never supplant the mages, they come in a very respectable second place.

Less than 1 child in 10,000 has the gift. Those who don't are pulled from the water, unconscious, lungs full of fluid. Resuscitation is attempted, vigorously, and is usually effective. But the children who become mages simply burn the water away with color fire.

For reasons the general populace don't quite understand, yellow or green are the most common colors of fire to erupt from children during the test.

Do these colors represent the common conceptions of fear or lack of experience (respectively)? No. The answer, as with many answers to life's mysteries, is much simpler. These colors fall near the middle of the spectrum and serve as a starting point.

Children who pass The Test and become apprentices are taken to the Atys Grand Conservatory for the Education, Indoctrination, and Development of Apprentices, commonly referred to as the GC. Even the very youngest children seen wearing the crest of the GC — a roaring head of a male lion with a mane of black fire — are given deference and respect on the streets of Atys. For no one ever knows how far along in training an apprentice might be. They each develop in their own time, some quickly, some taking longer. And therefore, no one ever knows exactly how dangerous any apprentice might be. It's infinitely safer to pay respects and keep your distance.

Color fire is not truly a fire, even though it burns. It is more like some kind of gelatinous substance that the apprentice or mage is able to produce from thin air. As a substance, it is finite and malleable. Each apprentice works to master the control of the substance, as well as to add more color to the 'fire.' When their color fire can spring forth as the purest black, the apprentice becomes a mage. A mage is able to produce fire of varied colors for various needs, but black represents the combinations of them all, and thus, the most powerful.

Purple fire is generally used in a healing capacity. It still burns, but the burn is controlled and more of a cauterizing effect. Meanwhile, red fire puts forth a much greater intensity of heat, creating the more standard definition of fire. It burns relentlessly. Combining these with yellow, green, and other parts of the spectrum, the purest black fire is the incarnation of death. Nothing in the Known World can withstand pure black fire.

Huldrych, by the strict definition of being able to produce black fire, therefore never truly graduated to become a mage. He learned new color fires, same as the other apprentices. But when he finally reached the Stage of Combination, when he put all his color fires together, the result was, to put it mildly, unexpected. White.

Of the people who were shocked by this result, Huldrych was the foremost. In fact, Huldrych was shocked to even find he could produce any color fire at all, never thinking of himself as particularly special. But, at age four, when his mother and father had thrown him kicking and screaming into the water and held him under while the village elders watched, Huldrych had indeed produced. His yellow fire, a particular yellow that some later said was unique as well, burned away the water and he stood, unharmed. By age eight, four years into his apprenticeship, he could produce most of the other colors. At ten, his first foray into the Stage of Combination produced white fire. His mage teachers weren't about to admit defeat at that time, though later they did. After eight more years of a dull and repetitive apprenticeship, one in which every attempt was made to switch off the white fire and somehow find the black, Huldrych was informed he should leave the GC. The citizens at large assumed, naturally, that this meant he was a mage. No one had ever left the GC before, in living memory or ancient texts, and *not* been a fully graduated mage.

But even the general populace could tell something was different about Huldrych. First, unlike most of the mages who either lived like kings in the city, or like lords of other cities, towns, and villages, Huldrych lived alone and lived simply, in a small hut nestled in the foothills outside of the remote village of Doa. Second, where every other known mage wore the flaming lion head of the Atys GC as a ring made of black onyx, Huldrych wore no ring at all.

Still, the mages had a reputation to uphold. So, on the remarkably few times when Huldrych was seen in public, the other mages were forced to nod and call him 'brother,' as they did to each other (unless of course the mage was female, in which case 'sister' was the proper address). Among the mages, power was the only commodity worth trading, and their primary task in life was to amass as much of the stuff as possible. While the general public knew a bit about their power struggles, internally mages were a backstabbing lot. The words 'brother' and 'sister' were spoken in so many different ways to connote myriad levels of respect, disdain, or indifference. But, when spoken to Huldrych, the word 'brother' took on an especially unpleasant air of disgust.

* * *

Two years into his post-apprenticeship exile, at the ripe age of twenty, Huldrych's only regular visitor was Corymna, a girl three years his junior and daughter of the main shopkeep of Doa. Corymna was pretty, gentle, patient, and generally ignored by the most of the other young eligible bachelors in Doa. This was for several reasons. First, she made no attempt whatsoever to 'pretty herself' for the purpose of finding a mate. Second, she spoke her mind. And finally, from the moment she saw Huldrych, she was in love, and so the affection of others in town was not only unwanted, it was a constant irritant. Corymna regularly went to some length to make herself less interesting. But, boys being boys, there was always some young fool interested in asking her to a dance, or to stroll by the stream, or what-have-you. The only boy, well, man, who never expressed any such interest was Huldrych. And that, of course, was enough to drive her mad.

For his part, Huldrych was not completely blind, not completely unaware of her interest, and not complete disinterested in her himself. In fact, he was more than 'not disinterested,' he was, in fact, quite interested. But he had been humiliated by his peers, and he was an outcast. These things took time to overcome.

When a rap came upon his door, Huldrych was deep in thought. But the possibility — nay, the near 100% likelihood — that it was Corymna drove him to his feet. He walked to the door and paused. For even he was aware that pretenses were somehow rigidly and stupidly important. He couldn't just swing open the door, like a gushing schoolboy, when Corymna appeared. He had to make her wait a bit. Settle himself. Be able to present himself calmly.

This is likely what saved his life.

For mages are simply human, and just as frail. Huldrych, less than a mage, was still equal to the task of being human. Which is to say, he was mortal and in danger. The rap came to his door, and at first he leaped to receive Corymna. But the rap, and it's strange how such a thing as a rap can have more than one meaning, seemed different. This was not

Corymna's knock. Not her thin wrist thrusting her tiny knuckles against the wood. This was more.

Huldrych waited, unsure.

Staying still, he tried to outlast his opponent. It wasn't hard. In general, people weren't patient. After only a moment or two, the person on his porch spoke. Meaning that it was not only one person on his porch: it was at least two.

"You said he was home," said one, muffled to Huldrych's ears through the door.

"I said I *thought* he was home," the other replied.

There was a *harrumph*. "You're a bit of an idiot, aren't you?"

"Who's the bigger idiot? Me or those who follow me?"

A thud sounded and a gasp. "You watch it or I'll do you in," said a voice, probably the second.

"Well," said the first slowly, "if he ain't here, he can't stop us from having a look around."

A pause. "True, good thought. Let's."

The door shivered, and the knob jiggled. Huldrych waited. He knew it was truly unfair what was about to happen. He pictured it in his head. The door, lock picked, would swing open, and the two would see him standing there. Enraged, or stupid, or brave, or whatever, they would attack. And Huldrych would unleash his fire, and they would die. Yes, his fire was white, and not the all-powerful black fire. But it killed, just the same.

He didn't want that to happen. In the moment of being robbed, he felt bad for his hapless opponents.

He leaned forward and unlocked the door, then stepped out onto the porch.

The two men staggered, unsure. One raised a club.

Huldrych wagged a finger at them. "Tsk tsk," he said. "Stop that. Or…" He pointed that single finger, lowering it slowly to point at a small pine just off the porch. Giving one last look at the two would-be thieves, he wiggled the end of his finger. And white fire sprang forth, incinerating the small tree.

The two stood motionless. After a moment, Huldrych realized they weren't even breathing. Then one of the men turned his head slowly toward the husk of the tree. And he ran. Within a moment, the second followed.

Huldrych walked to the wooden bench on his porch and plopped himself into it, exhausted despite having done little. His chin dipped down to his chest and he sat, alone and motionless, as the pine needles burned.

* * *

Some time later, Huldrych realized he was not alone. Someone was standing beside him. Upset with himself for letting the bad men return without noticing, he lifted his finger, at the ready. And he heard a feminine gasp.

Immediately, he lowered his guard. Shaking his head to clear his vision, he realized who was beside him. "Corymna! Apologies. When did you arrive?"

"Just now. I…" she paused, looking around with wide eyes. "I saw the smoke, the tree smoldering, then I saw you here and thought you might be… dead."

"No, no, no, just resting. Again, apologies," he said. He looked to the road, seeing if she had brought provisions. It was another of the gestures of the mages. Not out of charity, pity, or a genuine desire to help. But a means to an end. The mages provided Huldrych with sufficient supplies so that he felt no compulsion to announce in public that the GC was not 100% foolproof. But, on this day, there was no cart in the road. There were no provisions. So, why was Corymna on his porch?

She was, it appeared, absolutely not there to restock his supplies.

He looked her in the eye and saw she was restless, fidgeting. "What is it, Corymna?" he asked.

"I've been asked to bring you back to town," she said, simply. It was one of the things he liked most about her. In no way did the architecture of conversation ever get in the way of the meaning. She said what she meant, and he enjoyed it. Unlike the complex, nuanced relationship he had with the mages, his conversations with Corymna were easy to understand.

But he considered her words a moment. "Asked?" he replied. "Who asked you?"

"Radchina. There were three others with her, but Radchina did the asking."

Huldrych was taken aback. "Really?" He sat in stunned silence for a while. "What does Radchina want with me? In fact, why does Radchina even know I exist?"

Corymna blinked. "What do you mean?"

For a moment he forgot that she was a common citizen and, at least in her mind, he was a powerful mage. When it dawned on him, he lowered his head for a moment. "Apologies again, honored Corymna. Radchina is well above my station, as you might have noticed," he waved a hand at his surroundings, the lonely little hut. "I did not expect to receive her attention."

Corymna nodded in understanding. "Nor did I expect her in my home. Nor did my father. But she came, with the others. It is unheard of. She asked me to seek you out, so here I am. Will you come?"

Four mages superior had come looking for him? Huldrych locked eyes when Corymna for a moment or two longer, then nodded.

* * *

Slightly more than two hours later, Huldrych followed Corymna into her father's home.

"They're gone," said Yash, Corymna's wealthy father. Huldrych waited for more information without requesting it. It said something about the state of the world that the lowliest of mages (or even one who wasn't really a mage) could silently make demands of the most powerful businessman in the town. "Back to Atys. They said they would wait for you at the GC."

Huldrych grimaced, looking as if he was about to spit on the floor. But he remembered his host, and more importantly, that his host was the father of a daughter he held in high esteem. "This better be for a very good reason," he growled.

* * *

Doa was, intentionally as far as Huldrych was concerned, quite some distance from Atys. Color fire, although powerful, did not have any ability to alter space or time, so Huldrych was forced to walk or find a ride. Thankfully, he had money, so Yash was able to secure a carriage. But it was two days before Huldrych would even see the outskirts of Atys, another half day to the GC. He cursed, thinking of the abject boredom of the trip. And, of course, he considered his options.

First, he could ignore the call. But since he had already walked to Corymna's house, even he couldn't suddenly pretend he wasn't interested in what Radchina had to say.

Second, he could take the journey, be miserable and bored, and most likely come away even more upset. For what could Radchina truly want with him? He expected nothing but veiled or even direct insults and some sort of ridiculous waste of his time.

Finally, he could do something completely different. He had the carriage. He could leave. Set up a life again, somewhere new. Hope to avoid the long shadow of the mages this time.

But...

Huldrych blinked, turning his head to where she stood. Corymna wiped her hands on one length of her dress, maintaining a worried expression. And he had to admit. He wanted to see her again.

"I'll be back when it's done. Whatever it is," he said with resignation, climbing into the carriage. Yash nearly shrugged, not terribly anxious to ever see the young, reclusive mage again. Corymna simply watched. The sendoff was less than majestic.

And so the carriage slowly rolled forward, leaving Doa behind and seeking Atys ahead.

* * *

Two days later, Huldrych felt the carriage stop at the crest of a hill. It shook a bit as the driver jumped down. He heard words, nothing clear. Finally, the door swung open. "Sir… you… it's…" The driver paused a moment to gather himself. "Please come out."

Huldrych slowly put aside his reading, tucking it back into the single bag he'd brought. Outside, there was some strange noise. He dropped down to the ground, leaving the relatively dark interior to step out into the sun.

Huldrych reached for his back, sore from the long ride. He stretched, bending slowly backward, leaning up toward the bright sky. It took him a moment for his eyes to adjust.

In the distance, where Atys, the most powerful capital city in the Known World stood, there was smoke.

After a moment in which he again considered his options, Huldrych spoke. "Get me there quickly," he told the driver.

* * *

The heavy iron gates of the GC swung open, their oversized flaming lion heads roaring silently forever. The carriage passed through and into the courtyard. It was a place Huldrych had hoped to never see again, given that he spent fourteen mostly-miserable years of his life there. But in another way, he was home. Despite the humiliation of failure, despite the anger at being cast out, he had lived more than two-thirds of his life in this place. He couldn't deny the comfort he felt in returning.

A single apprentice was sent running out to meet him. *Just one*, he thought. *Yet another sign of disrespect.* The driver passed Huldrych's few bags to the apprentice, then stood waiting for his tip. Huldrych gave over a few of his larger gold coins. He knew it was far more than the man expected, and saw the driver's eyes go wide. "Thank you, sir. Should I wait for you nearby, in case you wish to return to Doa?"

Huldrych thought a moment. He plucked another of the large coins out of his purse and handed it to the driver. "Yes. Good idea. I hope this will be brief." Then he turned and followed the apprentice up the wide steps to the massive entrance to the GC's Great Hall. "What's your name?" he asked the boy.

"Allanth, sir," the boy said, hushed and reverent. *At least he's not disrespecting me. Yet,* Huldrych thought.

"Well, Allanth, before we go in, I will need a place to refresh myself. I've been traveling for days. Take me to the Guest Halls." Allanth froze, nervously.

"Ye — yes, sir," he said, changing direction. As he led Huldrych into the Guest Halls, a startled hall manager nearly fell out of his chair. "The Respected Mage Huldrych seeks a room to refresh himself," Allanth announced.

The hall manager, an older man, grey-haired and pudgy, looked first at Allanth, then Huldrych, then back to the boy. *Clearly he knows enough to know I'm no mage*, Huldrych thought. Still, it was unlikely the manager would attempt to deny them. Sure enough, he walked behind his desk, fumbled for some keys, and led them wordlessly to a room. Huldrych noticed as they passed several doors, knew enough of the place to know he was not being taken to the best room. *Perhaps the best rooms are already full*, he thought, knowing that not to be true.

After helping place his bags in the room, the apprentice Allanth was restless. Huldrych knew the poor boy was torn. Stay and risk the wrath of all the mage superiors, or leave and risk angering this new one. He had no wish to torture the child, so he waved him off and watched as Allanth ran back up the hall toward the exit. He already knew the boy's destination: the Great Hall, where he would tell the superiors that Huldrych had snubbed them, for now. Of course he wouldn't use those words, but they would know just the same.

* * *

Less than an hour later, a knock came at the door. "Yes?" Huldrych called out.

Allanth's voice replied. "Respected Mage Huldrych, sir. Mage Superior Gerring is with me and wishes to speak to you." *Well, that's a little better*, Huldrych thought, rising to open the door.

"Mage Superior, thank you for visiting me," he said with a smile. Gerring was one of the mage superiors, but far from the top. Radchina was above him in station, but even she was not truly in charge. Dozens of mage superiors served as a sort of king's court for the one in command: Grand Mage Besheam Lem. In Huldrych's lifetime, in all the years he walked these very corridors, he had seen Grand Mage Besheam Lem only twice, and both times from very far away.

Mage Superior Gerring wordlessly dismissed Allanth, who left and closed the door behind him, leaving them alone. "Huldrych," he began. *No pleasantries there*. "You've been summoned here by Mage Superior Radchina and a group of other mage superiors, including myself. I will not insult either your intelligence or mine to say this was not a difficult thing to do. We both know you did not leave this place with honor." Huldrych grimaced ever so slightly at the sting of it being said out loud. "Nevertheless, we have a need. You've no doubt seen our city has met with attack?" Huldrych nodded. "Come with me to the Great Hall, that Mage Superior Radchina and the rest of our group may explain our plight." It was only barely a request.

"What of the Grand Mage? Does he know I've been summoned here?"

Gerring cleared his throat roughly. "He does. But he chooses to recuse himself of this business. For now." *So, whatever it is they want me for, it hasn't been by unanimous decision.* Huldrych nodded, and Gerring opened the door. In the hallway, Allanth bowed and lead the way back to the Great Hall.

* * *

The Great Hall of Atys Grand Conservatory could easily hold well over a thousand people inside its massive walls, and in fact was often overflowing with mages on days of important ceremony. Allanth waited outside as Huldrych followed Gerring through the doors and down the long rows of chairs. At first he saw no one. Then he realized his mistake: there were mages present. Exactly five, nearly hidden in their ornate dark wooden seats at the far end of the room. A sixth stood motionless at the left side of the raised dais: Radchina herself.

Mages, in general, followed no specific dress code. Other than the black lion ring, they seemed like any other human, excepting of course for their undeniable air of superiority. As Gerring reached the front of the hall, he turned left and sat next to two colleagues. Huldrych stood at the end of the central aisle, three mages superior to his left, three to his right, and Mage Superior Radchina in front of him. Years melted away, and for a moment he felt he was back in his apprenticeship, chastised once again for his inability to produce black fire. He stood, awaiting whatever Radchina had to say.

She turned, her long black dress flowing behind her. Though the mages wore what they pleased, black was not an uncommon color. Whether it was a personal preference or some fashion, Huldrych had no idea, but of course he assumed it was a public reminder of their abilities. Still, glancing to each side, he noted the other mages superior wore browns, reds, whites, and one even sported a bright blue embroidered jacket. He looked at his own plain, rough-woven clothing, feeling all eyes upon him.

"Huldrych, thank you for coming at my request," Radchina said, shattering the heavy still silence in the air of the Great Hall. Her words echoed faintly behind him. In response, he said nothing, but dipped his head slightly with what he thought was a reasonable but not excessive show of respect. "You know we're under attack. And no doubt you know that the mages of Atys have come under attack hundreds of times before and prevailed. In fact, of those times, only seven times has any attacker breached the city walls." Huldrych had fourteen years of history lessons mixed into his training at the GC. He didn't need her summary, but let her continue without interruption. "Those seven instances have been studied in great detail, allowing the mages to be even more prepared in the face of each new attack. The last such time was over one hundred years ago, when the Fallan Aga hordes used clever tactics to come at us from nearly all directions at once. Given the power of black fire, the mages typically defended the city by brute force, thwarting all comers, but the Fallan Aga reminded us that we need to work together."

Huldrych remained silent. This was clearly not why he had been asked to come. The Fallan Aga had been utterly destroyed after gaining their entrance to the city. Once the mages realized they were truly in danger, their coordinated counterattack was unstoppable. Not a single Fallan Aga lived, according to the history books. Huldrych nodded impatiently, and Radchina could see she had made enough of her point.

"We now face a much greater problem. A problem unique in the thousand years history of our city and our kind. For the past twenty-three days, we have been attacked, quite randomly, by creatures we have never encountered before. A race that calls themselves the Ku Suru."

A long silence followed. Clearing his throat, Huldrych asked without preamble, "Is this why you wished me to come?" Radchina slowly nodded. "Then what is it about this new threat, these Ku Suru, that makes you contact me? After all, the last time I was in this place, the mages superior asked me to leave. Demanded I leave. Even demanded I never speak of the failures that happened within these walls." The words made Radchina and the others cringe, and Huldrych felt the slightest bitter joy at being able to make them uncomfortable.

"Huldrych, all that you say is true. But it is also true that we simply don't understand why you could never attain black fire. And that is the real reason you are here." Again she paused.

Sighing, Huldrych spoke again. "With all due respect, Mage Superior, say what it is you mean to say."

"The Ku Suru, our new enemy, can *absorb* black fire."

Huldrych drew in a long breath. *Absorb black fire?* He found it near impossible to believe.

"And because of this, their attacks have been very... successful." Radchina swallowed visibly, a nervous sign Huldrych had never seen any mage exhibit before. "We've lost some of our own," she admitted.

"How many?" he asked with surprise.

Radchina stared at him with her dark brown eyes, piercing. He knew that what she was saying was a tempest of emotions for her: fear, humiliation. "Hundreds."

Huldrych gasped. *"Hundreds?"* For the first time, he considered where he was, what was truly happening.

He had been dragged into a war where mages were being slaughtered. And, as far as the enemy was concerned, he probably looked an awful lot like a mage himself. "What exactly do you expect *me* to do about this?" he asked incredulously.

Radchina, seemingly having said the worst of it, gathered herself, standing straighter. "You need to know that all is not lost. We *can* defeat them, though it is tricky and becomes trickier with each loss of a mage. The Ku Suru can not only absorb black fire, they can absorb all colors of fire. But..." She let the word hang. "They cannot absorb *two* colors at the same time. We have been able to kill them when two mages work together, one spouting black fire, and the other using any other color. The Ku Suru seem to be able to nearly instantly tune their bodies to one color, but cannot take two at once."

"Then just hit them that way, you don't need me for that!" Huldrych said emphatically.

"I wish it was that simple. You see, they are many. And we are fewer and fewer. They appear unannounced, several at a time, from someplace unknown. They slaughter the citizens like goats, if for no other reason than to bring us out. It is possible they shift space to appear where they wish, when they wish. We can't be prepared with multiple mages in all places at all times."

"But you can ensure that mages always travel together, even bed near each other, so that no single mage is caught by surprise," he offered.

"Yes, and we have done so. But again, they attack in groups. Two mages together is enough to kill one of the Ku Suru at a time, without fail. But when there are three or four Ku Suru at once, and only two mages? Our numbers are dwindling."

"So…" Huldrych knew what would come next. "You want me to try my white fire." It wasn't a question. Radchina, Gerring, and the rest nodded in unison.

"We feel we must at least ask you to try, yes. Grand Mage Besheam Lem is not convinced, but even he is desperate enough to let us contact you."

"And what if I say no?" he asked, hardly able to believe he was standing up to seven mages superior on the very floor of the Great Hall. His knees quivered slightly, and he hoped none of them saw.

Radchina shrugged. "We will continue to fight. We will do our best, but we may well lose. Then the mages will be gone. You can go back into exile, but the Ku Suru came to us, from wherever they are born. They may find you one day, too." Huldrych could tell right away that Radchina had finally said all she intended to say. Her argument, in total, was out, and he had to decide.

They slaughter the citizens like goats, he thought, then imagined Corymna as one of the Ku Suru's hapless victims.

"I will try. Take me where I need to go."

Radchina huffed. "There is nowhere to go. They will appear when and where they wish. All we can do is wait."

There was not so much as a thank you.

* * *

He only had to wait a day.

Mage Superior Gerring got the auspicious duty of being paired with Huldrych. On their panel of seven, they broke into twos for safety, leaving Gerring out. In a way, Gerring almost seemed glad to have someone to pair with, even if that someone was an outcast without black fire.

Given this time together, Huldrych quizzed Gerring on the Ku Suru, trying to learn as much as there was to know. There wasn't much.

As Radchina had said, the Ku Suru were many. They appeared where and when they desired, without warning. And they absorbed all color fire, though only one color at a time. Their physical appearance was similar to a large human warrior, and they wore thick armor. But their skin was the palest white any mage had ever seen or heard story of, so pale as to almost appear translucent, with their hair near white. Their armor was a light yellowish metallic color, with nasty spikes at various joints, and they wielded blades of a similar metal, the length equivalent to about three-quarters of their height. They attacked without mercy and apparently without fear, throwing themselves toward mages until one of their party would break through the counterattack and deal a fatal blow. They seemed to make a point of killing mages, as they would only kill citizens in order to draw the mages' attention. Once they succeeded in a fight, they would depart. They didn't hold onto any conquered land, nor indeed did they have any known base of operations. Citizens who had witnessed them killing mages reported that, just before departing, they would state in unison, "We are the Ku Suru. We will prevail." As for where they went, the citizens could only report that the attackers would step forward, seem to bend in some strange way, and disappear.

All of this information gave Huldrych a less than positive outlook for his continued survival. Being back at the GC, a place where for years he was deemed an utter failure, did little to improve his disposition.

But when the attack came, there was very little time to worry about such things.

Just before falling asleep, the evening after his meeting with Radchina in the Great Hall, Huldrych was lying in bed. He could hear Gerring already lightly snoring across the room when suddenly there was a yelp from out in the hall.

Huldrych sat up. Another sound, a loud clang, roused Gerring. Then a shout. It was Allanth. "Mages! Help!" Quickly, they rushed out into the hall.

And toward the main entrance, they saw Allanth cornered by the imposing form of a Ku Suru warrior, his long blade hung above the cowering apprentice. Allanth raised one hand in desperation, firing off a yellow stream of color fire into the belly of the attacker. Huldrych watched the Ku Suru warrior's pale skin turn the faintest yellow color as it absorbed the fire. Then it swung the blade.

"No!" Huldrych shouted, and white fire flew from his fingers. It connected with the warrior's core, just where Allanth's yellow fire was still being absorbed. And the Ku Suru burst into flames, screaming, and fell.

Allanth didn't waste time, jumping up and running down the hall toward the mages. Behind him, a second Ku Suru entered the hall, seemingly only barely able to fit its large form under the low roof. Instinctively, and out of personal fear, both Gerring and Huldrych shot color fire, black and white at the same time. The second Ku Suru fell, engulfed in flame.

And other than the sound of the dying, things went silent.

"Are there others?" Gerring asked Allanth in a whisper.

Allanth nodded, clearly terrified. "I think there were three. One of them killed the hall manager!"

Gerring cursed. "Then where is the other bastard?" As if in response, they saw movement, out past the entrance to the hall, in the main room.

The Ku Suru appeared, standing its ground, seeming to wait. Gerring raised one hand, but Huldrych covered it with his own.

"No. Let me try alone. That's why you brought me here, right?" Gerring nodded, lowering his hand almost with relief as Huldrych stepped forward. The Ku Suru didn't move.

Not used to killing in cold blood, Huldrych paused. "What is it you want? Why have you come?"

"We are the Ku Suru. We will prevail." It was the warrior's only response.

"So I've heard. But prevail for what purpose?" Huldrych stepped forward, into the main room, glad to be out of the low hallway. Behind him, Gerring waited by the threshold, with Allanth cringing behind. At least they could now see that there was only one Ku Suru left alive in the room.

Still, they fell back as the warrior suddenly sprang into action. It rushed forward, pulling its long metal blade back in preparation.

And Huldrych sent white fire in a thick, bright beam, directly into the Ku Suru's chest.

It was as if the pale skin of the warrior became even more pale, nearly pure white. It absorbed his white fire, and it kept coming. "It's not working!" Huldrych shouted as the Ku Suru's blade came arcing down toward him. He ducked left and rolled away as the blade dug into the carved wooden panels of the wall. Huldrych shot white fire again, this time at the back of the warrior. Still the fire was absorbed and the Ku Suru turned to face him again. It took a step toward him as he lay sprawled on the floor, still pointlessly pumping white fire into the warrior.

Suddenly the Ku Suru's skin took on a yellowish tint, and it burst into flame. It fell to the ground, writhing.

Behind the dying warrior, in the hallway entrance, Huldrych saw Allanth with one hand outstretched, the yellow color fire dissipating.

* * *

They gathered themselves in the main room, where the three Ku Suru lay dead. "What've we learned?" Huldrych said, mostly to himself.

"Learned?" Gerring said indignantly. "We've learned *nothing*. Or worse than nothing. What we've learned is that you're just as useless as we thought all those years." He scoffed and turned away.

He has a point. White fire didn't work, Huldrych thought. *We had to use two fires to bring them each down.* He considered what he had seen, but nothing of use came to mind. Still, something bothered him that he couldn't quite place.

"Sirs. Let us help. Just like I did tonight. I know my fellow apprentices want to help you," Allanth offered.

Huldrych nodded. "That's a good thought. It really doesn't matter what color fire is used, we just need more than one."

"Which means we're in the same position as before you arrived, only slightly improved if we use the apprentices," Gerring said. "Rather than die next week, now we might last a month." He threw up his hands in frustration and anger.

"Still, we should go talk to Radchina and the others. Get them to rally the apprentices. It might just gain us a few weeks, but that could be time we need," Huldrych said, still thinking.

"We need for what?" Gerring asked, mockingly.

"To think of something totally new."

* * *

The three walked across the dark courtyard toward the Great Hall. The mages superior wouldn't be there so late at night, but they would be summoned by the guards on duty. It would be quicker than seeking each mage out in his or her own room.

As the moon beamed down on them, partially obscured behind a cloud, they reached the middle of the courtyard. And quickly realized they were not alone.

Like seeing something out of the corner of his eye then turning to bring it in focus, Huldrych watched three Ku Suru appear before him, blocking the way. The warriors didn't hesitate; there seemed no point in discussion or negotiation. As the three Ku Suru ran toward them, Huldrych, Gerring, and Allanth sent color fire toward their attackers, turning them each into a burning, charred mass. Huldrych released his tension and stood taller, turning toward the others, just as a Ku Suru crashed into the three of them from behind, sending Allanth flying across the courtyard. The apprentice hit his head, hard, against the stone pavers and didn't move again. Gerring and Huldrych shot their fires at the warrior and he burned. But turning, they saw there were more. Too many more. They would be overwhelmed for certain.

Huldrych's mind raced. How could they destroy so many, when they both needed to attack in unison to produce two colors?

Wait, he thought.

"Wait," he said aloud. Gerring looked at him.

"Wait for what? To die? We need to fire together, *now*!" He shot his black fire forth and it was absorbed by every Ku Suru it touched. Huldrych's fire remained absent.

"Try to fire two colors at once. Like when we were in the Stage of Combination, in our apprenticeship. But try to keep them apart." He dared smile.

Gerring thought Huldrych had cracked from the pressure. "It's impossible," he said.

"Just *try*," Huldrych replied.

Gerring raised his hand, and a blaze of red fire shot forth, easily absorbed by the approaching warriors. Then, in his mind, he began to think of blue. He raised his other hand. And new flames erupted from those fingers as well. But their color was purple, and instantly the color coming from his other hand turned purple as well. The purple color fire swept across the approaching front lines of Ku Suru, and was absorbed. "I told you, it's impossible!" he yelled, stepping backward.

Huldrych raised one hand and red fire erupted. Quickly, seeing the Ku Suru closing in, he raised his other hand and he too began to think of blue. Both hands shot fire, and those colors instantly combined. But where Gerring's red and blue formed purple, Huldrych's fire ran magenta.

Still it was absorbed.

They had no choice. They swept their two fires across the approaching warriors, killing them by the dozens. But it only bought them a little time. Many more Ku Suru appeared to take their fallen comrades' places, folding out of space or time and into existence in the courtyard.

"Our only hope is to alert the others! We need more mages!" Gerring shouted.

"There has to be some way," Huldrych said to himself, lost in thought, mind racing. Gerring turned and ran toward the Great Hall.

Right in front of Gerring, space folded and a Ku Suru appeared. Instinctively, Gerring shot black fire, but Huldrych had no time to help. The yellow blade of the Ku Suru cut Gerring down mercilessly, and he fell, bleeding hideously.

More Ku Suru began to appear. Huldrych was fully surrounded. And now he was alone.

Something in his mind *itched*. There was something in there, something special about his color fire. When Gerring shot red and blue, it made purple. When Huldrych did the same, it was magenta. What if Gerring had tried yellow and red? Orange. How about red and green? *What would that become?* Huldrych though, hopping quickly from idea to idea, knowing the Ku Suru were closing around him.

For Gerring, that'd be grey, I think. The mages' color fires ran to black when they combined them in various ways, even the complimentary colors.

But what about *his* fire? What would red and green look like together if Huldrych combined them? He had never tried.

The Ku Suru around him shouted in unison and ran, closing fast. He had seconds to live.

And so he sent red fire and green fire forth from his hands. And they could not combine. For there was no red-green. It was *no* color, it could not be made. It was an *impossible* color.

The red was there, and so was the green, together, in the same place at the same time, though it defied all reason. And it cut down the Ku Suru one and all. Huldrych spun around, wild red-green, impossible color fire burning the attackers. More and more came, but still the red and green came from his hands. And still they died.

Then it stopped. The Ku Suru lay dead, or dying. Huldrych stood, panting from the effort, disbelieving.

Turning about, looking for any remaining opponent, Huldrych saw several mages slowly appear, drawn by the commotion. Radchina herself stepped out from a doorway. "Huldrych, how?" She looked around, amazed. "We heard the fighting and came. We saw what you did. But… how?" she repeated.

Huldrych just sighed.

And then, on the far side of the courtyard, the air seemed to fold, and a single Ku Suru appeared. It held its long blade low, and did not attack. It stood looking at Huldrych for a long moment. Though exhausted, he tensed, hands coming up, ready.

"We are the Ku Suru. We will prevail," the warrior said, then it folded and disappeared.

* * *

"We owe you our sincerest apologies." Grand Mage Besheam Lem spoke in a dignified tone from atop the dais.

Huldrych had been asked to come to the Great Hall, and although he wanted to be away from the place, away from the GC, he agreed. Every mage in the city was in attendance, with Huldrych given a seat of honor in the first row, along the center aisle.

It was a sad sight that nearly half of the Great Hall stood empty. They had lost that many.

"Mage Superior Radchina suggested we find you, and so she should be the one to speak to you now." Grand Mage Besheam Lem stepped aside, sitting near the back of the dais on the right. Mage Superior Radchina took his place in the center, standing, wearing a long green dress. Huldrych was mildly surprised she wasn't in black.

"Huldrych, it is nothing less than the truth to say you have saved the city, saved the mages," she smiled at him. "We cannot thank you enough." The mages applauded loudly until Radchina raised one hand to quell them. "We know that you spent many long years at this institution, and that you left in disgrace, without graduation to the level of mage. We fully admit our error. Respected Mage Huldrych, you have more than earned your place among our ranks." More applause. Huldrych's cheeks went red. He expected their thanks, their kudos, but he really hadn't expected this. To be made a mage? It was both an honor and a keen reminder of their previous disrespect.

Still, he nodded, allowing himself to smile. Fourteen years he had been in this place and failed. It felt good to succeed.

"But there is one more thing we wish to ask of you, Respected Mage Huldrych." The smile faded from his face. *What now?* "You have done something no one else has done, not any of the mages around you, nor anywhere in the recorded histories. Will you stay and teach us?"

In the society of mages, purity of ability was the ultimate virtue, and this purity came from knowledge. To be asked to teach the mages was therefore the highest compliment that could possibly be bestowed upon Huldrych. If his cheeks had appeared red before, they were bright crimson now.

Radchina awaited his response. Slowly Huldrych stood, looking around across all the waiting faces of the mages, now his true brothers and sisters.

But he couldn't help still feeling like the outcast. One accomplishment, no matter how large, couldn't erase the years of disconnect, the many snubs, the feelings of resentment at being cast out for something beyond his control. He looked down at his shoes. His plain shoes, and his plain clothing.

"Mage Superior Radchina, and all of my fellow mages…" The words felt awkward on Huldrych's lips. "No, I'm sorry. I don't belong here," he said. As the gathered mages gasped in unison, including the Grand Mage himself, Huldrych continued. "But do not take this as a sign of disrespect. I simply believe there is no way for me to teach you, just as there was no way for you to teach me, all of those years. Can an apple be taught to be an orange? I fear that, while we share many similarities, we are fundamentally different. Still…" He gazed around at the faces of the mages, seeing their renewed fear. "I realize the enemy is still out there, though we have no idea in what numbers. Many, many Ku Suru fell in the courtyard. But in time, they may attack again. I will return if I am needed."

Huldrych saw the disappointed look on Radchina's face, and although the Mage Superior was an attractive woman, he thought instead of Corymna. *I think I will ask her to have dinner with me when I get back,* he mused.

⊙

All That You Know is Lost and Abandoned

"I don't like horror," the girl said.

"Do you like life?" he replied.

"What?" she asked, turning toward him with her head tilted in confusion.

"Do you like life?"

"Well, that's either a really stupid or really scary question," she said after a moment.

"Why?" he asked.

"Because," she looked into his eyes, a doe-eyed expression that he assumed was meant to make him fall in love with her. It sort of worked. "Either I like life, like any living being wants to be alive, making that question really stupid, or somewhere inside me, I despise life, I want to die, and that's pretty scary. If not for me, at least for people close to me. Like you." She was practically batting her eyelashes at him.

"You didn't answer, though," he noted.

She sighed. "Fine. Yes."

"Yes, what? Yes, you like life, or yes, I'm stupid, or yes, you're scary, or —"

She cut him off. "Yes, I like life. Why the hell did you ask that, anyway?"

"Because you said you didn't like horror," he replied.

A moment passed.

"Did I miss something?" she asked.

"No."

"Okaaay…" She looked out the window for a moment, then turned back. It was hot in the car. The orange and yellow landscape blurred as it rushed by.

"Look, you asked me if I liked horror movies and I said no. Is that really such a big deal?" She waited, looking at the side of his head as he stared forward. "Okay, I admit it. I don't get it," she said.

"Get what?" he asked, idly steering. From her point of view, the sun turned him into a dark splotch, almost a silhouette. The light glinted off his metal-rimmed sunglasses.

She punched his arm, playfully. "You know what I'm saying. I don't get what you're talking about. What does liking life have to do with horror?"

He shrugged. "Life *is* horror."

"What?" She laughed a little laugh, looking off at the dry dust plains outside. Finally, she turned, expecting him to be laughing, too, but he wasn't. "Shut up. You're serious?"

"Yeah."

"How so?"

"You ever watch TV?" he asked, only glancing at her momentarily while driving the car.

"Um, yeah. You know this. What's the point?"

"Watch the news?"

"Also yes. Come on, tell."

"Ever see anything horrifying on the news?"

"Pretty much every day," she said, exasperated.

"Then there you go. Life is horror."

She sat waiting. After a moment, he little smile faded. "You know what? I want to change my answer."

"Answer to what?"

"Your question about life."

"Okay, what's your new answer?" he asked.

"My new answer is yes, you are stupid." She turned away, slightly annoyed, but thinking that at least this passed the time. Even driving fast, the ride was long.

He laughed. "Point taken," he said.

"Are you going to tell me what the hell you're talking about?" she asked. "Or have you gone crazy from driving too long? Need a switch?" She made a back-and-forth gesture with her hands.

"I told you: Life is horror," he repeated.

She just sighed, looking back out the window.

He heaved a sigh at having to explain. "Every day on TV, you see people dying. People losing loved ones, houses burning down, war, rape, murder, acts of depravity. Shameful, horrible things. Right?"

"Thanks for the pick-me-up," she scoffed.

"Right?"

"Of course, yes. People are shits and people do shitty things. And it's all on the nightly news. And the radio, and the Internet, blah blah blah."

"So that's horror," he said.

"I agree, it's horrible. But that doesn't make it *life*."

"Then what is it?"

"It's what terrible people do."

"War?"

"Yes."

"What if our country is at war? Are we then terrible people?"

"Can we change the subject?" she asked.

"No. Because it's not just terrible people, it's everyone. You're not a terrible person because your house burned down. You're not a terrible person because you were driving down the road and some asshole sheered your car in half, tearing you apart. But what happened was horrible. Horror is everywhere, every day."

"Okay, fine, I agree. Horrible things happen all the time in life. But there is a big difference between life, even with horrors, and a *horror movie*."

"If you say so," he said.

"You don't agree?" she asked smugly. "So you're saying that a supernatural homicidal maniac can be shot, stabbed, burned alive, drowned, and fall out of a twelve-story window, and still get up and try to stab you with a giant kitchen knife?"

"No," he chuckled. "*That* is definitely fiction."

"There!" she exclaimed.

The car slowed as he took his foot off the gas, turning toward her, distracted by her. "There, what?" he asked.

"That's why I don't like horror."

He considered her words for a moment, then put his foot down again, making the car resume speed. "But that's not the only kind of horror there is. I'm not talking about that supernatural kind. To me, that's more comedy."

"You're sick."

He shrugged. "Maybe. But the kind *you're* talking about is so ridiculous that I can't help but laugh."

"Yep. Sick," she said.

"Seriously, hear me out. What is *really* more horrifying? A supernatural killer who can survive any ridiculous attempt to kill him, who keeps coming at you, probably with a simple *knife*. I mean, really, these guys don't even get creative. Try lasers or smart bombs or something. The kitchen knife thing… it's old." She stared at him a moment, until he noticed the heat of her eyes on the side of his head. "What?"

"Is there a time when you plan to make a point?" she asked.

He rolled his eyes. "Are you paying attention? I'm asking you a question. What's really more horrifying? The supernatural killer, or plain old death, war, sickness, suffering? The stuff that happens all around us, every day."

"That."

"What?"

"That. What you said." She looked out the window, away from him.

"Which one?"

"The second."

"Why?"

She whipped her head back, hair flying in an arc. "Why do you think?" she huffed. "That supernatural crap. You can laugh it off, ignore it. But…"

"But what?"

"That real life shit is *awful*. God, that can happen to *anyone*."

He paused. "So, do you like it?"

"Why the hell would I like it? It's all the worse things about life —"

"And yet, it is integral to life. Horror is a part of life, just like pleasure."

She was uneasy now. She looked around, wondering if this was leading to something. "Well, fine, but I don't have to like it. And I'm certainly not going to go looking for it."

He stayed quiet for a moment, letting her settle down. When he spoke again, it was in a low voice. Over the drone of the car engine, maybe she didn't even hear it. "Doesn't matter. It comes looking for you."

For most of their drive, the road was empty. But, as luck and fate and life would have it, at that moment a car appeared on the horizon driving toward them on the other side of the road. He slowed a bit, to look less conspicuous, but it didn't help. He could tell. She could tell. They both fell silent.

As the car passed on their left, they both forced themselves to look forward, thinking this would look natural. In actuality, it did the opposite. Only two cars on the road for miles around, and they didn't spare a glance at the other car?

He looked into the rearview mirror and saw the black and white patrol car slowing, then turning.

He didn't bother with subtlety anymore, pressing the gas pedal all the way down.

She gazed at him, long and hard. Again, he felt her stare, like warmth on the side of his face. He turned, without speaking, figuring she had something to say.

She glanced quickly over her shoulder, seeing the bits of rock and debris kicked up behind their car, the lights blazing behind.

"Are *we* terrible people?" she asked in a quiet, afraid voice.

He turned to face directly ahead again, drinking in the few moments when, despite the speed and situation, he could fade into a calmness. The road noise, the drone of the engine, the heat... he sat and let the stillness of motion envelop him.

And then, with a slow, deliberate nod, he slammed the wheel left, hard, sending the car flying off the road and into the depressed brown hardback beyond. He looked in the rearview, saw the patrol car racing to catch up through the flying dust.

He reached over to the glovebox, flipping it open to reveal the oily black gun. He was still focused on finding a path through the light brush, trying to avoid the random holes he assumed were there, and felt her hand on his.

"No," she said. "I've got it. You drive."

Tilting

"What can we do to help, Captain Morris?" Avery asked.

"Mo. Just Mo," the codger said in a slow voice, waving one weathered hand as he reached down toward the rocky beach. Mo lifted a thick braid of rope, a straight line running from the place where it was firmly anchored into the stony hillside behind us, out into the water. There, in the calm waters of morning, the line met a utilitarian aluminum fishing boat. As he pulled, the boat glided toward us.

Dave looked speculatively at the wooden dock that loomed above us to our left. "Why don't you just use the dock?" he asked.

Mo didn't pause from pulling the boat to shore. "We've got twenty foot tides here. Tie it up tight, it's hanging out of the water in eight hours. Tie it up loose, it gets beat to hell." He sounded as if he might've given this response a hundred times before.

We all nodded as if we completely understood. As if we city boys had any understanding of this place.

The boat ground to a stop on the beach, metal grumbling across rock, water sloshing away. But the sound seemed muffled. The mountains surrounding the bay were mostly invisible, lost in fog hovering a few hundred feet off the water's surface. The wet green walls of the mountains boxed us between the water and the fluffy white ceiling, muting the world. As vast as our field of vision was, it felt as constricted as a coffin.

Mo continued his prep work, hefting supplies aboard the ship as he stood in the frigid shallows in heavy green rubber boots. I looked at my wristwatch. 6:28am.

"You got somewhere better to be, Gary?" Avery jokingly chided, a huge grin on his face. Arms wide, he spun slightly, indicating the wondrousness of nature around us.

"Nah, man," I said, donning a smile. "This place is incredible." Still, I felt a little lost. Like I had no idea what I was doing.

Dave wordlessly helped the captain load the boat. A couple coolers, buckets with gear, several long rods, a waterproof sack, and two large tackle boxes. It seemed like a lot of stuff for a day-long fishing trip.

Mo held the boat, giving us a look. "Come on. Fish won't catch themselves." For a moment, I just stared, not knowing what was expected of me. Then Dave sloshed into the water and scrambled onto the boat. Avery followed. I guess I was expecting a ladder or something. Trying to hide my embarrassment, stepped into the water. Even through the thick rubber boots I had been given, the water was very, very cold.

Getting on the boat was a challenge. The lodge had decked us all out in foul weather gear, and the heavy rubber coat and pants I wore felt stiff to my unaccustomed body. As I flopped on board, my boots made dull clomps on the deck. I turned back to see Mo walking the boat away from the shore, still in the water himself. Once satisfied, he reached up toward the gunwale. I extended one hand in aid, but he either missed it or ignored it, climbing aboard with the ease of years of practice. The boat rocked in heavy arcs as he stepped into the cockpit.

I'd been on a boat more times than I could remember, but never like this.

Not this place. Not this type of boat.

* * *

Boating, to me, meant the Chesapeake. And only in summer. Hot breezes, tilting sailboats, avoiding nettles. Sure, a good portion of the estuaries around the bay were shallow and navigation there required some degree of caution. But the penalty for failure was typically light. Wait through the tide, or at worst, for a hand from the Coast Guard, while you sipped another Miller Lite. Whether you were a sailor or power boater, it was the same. Our boats were mostly white and made of fiberglass. Our water was shallow, blue-green, brackish, and 75 degrees. Our surroundings were marshlands and sea level conifers. And the next boater was likely so close by that you could simply wave to get their attention.

I blinked my eyes to refocus. This was no Chesapeake.

This was Alaska.

Even more, this was Kodiak. Remote, sparsely populated, and at the mercy of Mother Nature and the Pacific Ocean. The nearest "city" was Larsen Bay. Population: 87. Even it was many miles away and in a direction unknown to me.

The air temperature was somewhere in the low-40s, water temperature notably lower. The lodge estimated the water at 34 degrees. "So, ya know, you can try swimming, if you like," the lodge manager had said, smiling with typical droll Alaskan sense of humor.

The boat wasn't tiny, but it certainly wasn't all that big. Maybe 30 feet. It was homemade from sheets of aluminum welded together at the lodge itself, and the whole surface was unadorned mottled grey. I suppose it was when I heard 'homemade' that I began to worry. "How long's she been afloat?" I asked, trying to sound nonplussed.

"'Bout five and half years," Mo said, lowering the engine. The fact that it wasn't made yesterday stifled some of my worries.

Mo cautiously backed us out into the bay, avoiding the shallows by keeping the prop up until he was sure we had depth. Soon, he dropped into a forward gear and we were off, leaving a long V of wake behind us on the otherwise still water. An otter rolled underwater as we zipped past.

We did what tourists did in exotic places. We looked around, sometimes mouth agape, sometimes pointing out something to one another. As we went around a small rocky island, Dave announced that there were puffins. Avery spied two sea lions in the water before they darted away and out of view. The engine pumped out a loud, near-constant roar that made conversation difficult. But an excitement was building.

The whole trip was Dave's idea, which is sort of ironic, given that it was his last. Dave loved fishing for as long as I could recall, and even though neither Avery nor I were all that committed, Dave's enthusiasm was catching. He easily talked us into 'a manly adventure.' DC to Chicago, Chicago to Anchorage, Anchorage to Kodiak City, then pontoon plane from the city to the lodge. A meal, a night of trading fish stories with other visitors to the lodge, then sleep and early rising to meet Mo at the boat. It was the first day of ten we had planned.

Just as I had been on a lot of boats, it could also be said that I'd been fishing countless times. And yet, it could be easily said that I had virtually no knowledge of how to actually be a fisherman. I planned to go last and pay close attention. If I caught anything, that'd just be a bonus.

Turns out the lodge expects novices like me. I didn't even need to say a word. At our first stop, Mo slowed the boat to a crawl, then dropped to neutral. Casually striding to the bow, he lowered the anchor (also aluminum, I guessed by the identical mottled grey color). The chain rattled against the hull as the anchor descended. It seemed to take forever, clattering link by link overboard.

"How deep is it here?" Avery asked.

Mo stepped lightly back into the cockpit and checked his depth finder with a tap. "302," he said.

"Feet?" I couldn't keep the surprise out of my response. We couldn't have been more than a half-mile off shore. If it was 302 feet deep here, that meant the sharp angle of the mountains poking upward from the shore was mirrored underwater as well.

"Yeah, feet. But that's 'cause we're on the edge. Deeper still further out. Runs deep and cold here," Mo said as he cut the engine.

Dante noted nine levels of hell. I think there are more. 300 feet of 34 degree water sounds like a hell, no matter how beautiful the nearby surroundings look.

Yet things live in this water. Things even thrive in this water.

All morning, we motored, stopped, fished, motored, stopped, fished. Not surprisingly, Dave was the best. Dave hauled in halibut every several minutes. But he was judicious.

"What do people catch here?" he asked.

Mo considered it for a moment. Alaskans, I thought, moved at a much slower pace than what I was used to from DC. "We see 90 pounds or bigger pretty regularly," he said.

Dave grimaced. At the same moment, Avery started working his pole like he had a bite. Mine stayed motionless. "What d'ya think that one is?" Dave asked Mo, pointing to the catch he had just hauled to the surface.

Mo scoffed. "45. Maybe."

"And what's the bag limit here?" Dave asked. Sometimes I thought there was a lot more to Dave than I understood. For example: bag limit. I had no idea what that meant until Mo replied.

"Two," Mo said, flatly. "Per day." So the maximum number of halibut we'd be taking home from this day's trip would be six. I nodded to myself, absently understanding.

"Throw 'er back," Dave said without another thought. As Dave hauled the fish — a rather big one by my estimation — up next to the boat, Mo stepped in. Using a large net, he was able to raise the halibut out of the water and steady it just enough to remove the hook. Then he flicked at the net handle, turning it to allow the fish to swim off into the sea. Finally, he rebaited Dave's line and sent it swinging back, ready for a new attempt. On the other side of the boat, Avery was casting again, apparently having lost his previous near-catch.

"Your bait's gone, son," Mo said to Avery without even looking his direction. "Pull 'er up and let me fix it for you."

Dave stood with his back to us, staring off across the cold water to the rugged and foggy mountains beyond. "What's the lodge record?" he asked over one shoulder.

"278 and 5/8," Mo said without a moment's hesitation.

"That's a monster!" I blurted out. I thought of halibut as dinner plate sized, or more specifically, something on my dinner plate. Not something that outweighed me by 100 pounds.

Dave turned to face him. "That's awful specific. Who caught it?" he asked.

"Me, of course," Mo replied, cracking the first and last smile I'd ever see on his face.

* * *

We rocked idly back and forth, tilting on waters cold enough to freeze our bones. Around us, around the bay, there were rocky mountains coated in frosty evergreen. Yet all of that was dominated by the fog. It sat on the horizon in every direction like vulture on a tree branch, waiting for an opportunity. It hung above our heads, making the sun nothing more than a slightly lighter patch of the muted grey-white sky.

Still, like most tourists, especially groups of male adult friends trying to 'get away,' we came to ignore it all. The day's challenge was halibut, the prize was the biggest fish, and this bay was simply crawling with the things. We hauled up one after the other, my complete lack of fishing skill making no difference. I had bait. I had a hook. I could spin the reel. The halibut came up.

Sure, we had to work for some of them. The bigger ones could be ornery. But unless the hook accidentally slid out, we got our catch. Halibut, while delicious at dinnertime, are an exceedingly ugly specimen of fish. Flat, with an algae-like green-brown coloring on the top side, where their two eyes are, but white on the other.

The morning passed without incident.

Plenty of fish, plenty thrown back (Dave was adamant we kept only the biggest), and plenty of side bets and trash talk. Mo simply sat back and took it in, occasionally rebaiting a line. For the few fish we kept, Mo would stab them with a nasty-looking thick metal hook attached to a short pole. We'd snap photos of the triumphant fisherman with our phones as blood dripped from the hook, down the fish's body and onto the deck. Finally, the unlucky fish was tossed into the frosty hold.

With each rebait, cast, wait, reel, I felt more comfortable. I was in a land I knew almost nothing about, doing an activity that was potentially as far removed from my normal daily life as you could get, and still it became routine.

"Let's eat," Mo suddenly said. He walked to one of the coolers and pried it open. The cooler creaked its objection. Inside was a humble assortment of sandwiches in plastic bags, cans of soda, chips, and some fruit. In short, it looked like mom had made us lunch. Which she probably had. The lodge manager and his wife ran everything. Mo passed items around without concern for who wanted what. We got what we got. That seemed to be the way of things in Alaska: play with the cards you're dealt.

We sat on the gunwales, munching and dropping crumbs all over ourselves and the boat. Avery tossed a chip overboard and let it float away. After a few moments, we saw it blink out of view, taken by some hungry fish. I downed a gulp of my cola and noticed Dave smiling.

* * *

David Murano had been one of my best friends for going on fifteen years. We'd met in middle school, sitting next to each other in class. Think about that for a second. How many times do life-long friends meet each other because they happened to live in the same school district, and some administrator randomly paired them into a class together? Anyway, once we reached our late twenties and had the usual assortment of adult commitments forming, we often spoke of having more exotic adventures. We both had growing careers, and Dave was married, no kids (though I fully expected him and his wife Molly to announce a pregnancy at any time). Dave had already attained the status of Vice President of Marketing for a small local firm. The firm hoped to have him forever, but Dave was likely to be snapped up by a bigger fish within twelve months. He was gregarious and outgoing, loved to camp, hike, and fish, and while he was deeply devoted to Molly, he definitely set aside time for us boys. Our previous trip had been to Vegas, and, while fun, we'd done that enough for the time being. Dave was the planner among us. And as such, he planned things that he liked. Like fishing trips in remote places.

Dave also was — how do I put this appropriately — the least lazy of us? If we all saw a 90 year old woman carrying bags of groceries to her car, we'd all think she needed help, but Dave actually would help her.

Who knew that was a bad character trait?

* * *

After lunch, we raised the anchor — and when I say 'we' here, I mean Mo, the captain. Really, the day was his, not ours. I couldn't tell you where we went or what our next destination was. I just knew we sped across the water for a little while, then we stopped and fished.

As we coasted into our next spot, I noticed something odd on the shore. Some sort of marker. It was nondescript, only standing out because it seemed clearly man-made, in stark contrast to everything else around us except the grey metal boat we stood upon.

"What's that?" asked Avery, seeing it, too.

"ADF&G marker," Mo replied.

"Of course," Avery replied sarcastically.

Mo shrugged off the insult. "Alaska Department of Fish and Game. The marker means commercial fishing boats can't go inland past this point."

"So does that mean the good fishing's out here?" Dave asked, with what sounded like envy.

Mo looked around, shrugging his shoulders. "Fish..." He made a wavy gesture with on hand. "They move around." It was all he had to say on the topic. After a pause, he changed the subject back. "Round here, we generally think the markers are the outer edge for small boats like ours. Plus, you see that fog rolling in as well as I do." He gestured toward the north.

"You mean go back?" Dave asked.

"Yeah, I mean go back. Just a bit, inside the markers. Safer for you, better for me. Listen. When you live in Alaska, you know it's beautiful, and you know it's deadly. You know that viewing nature from afar is sometimes the best plan, but you don't use that as a cop out. Regardless of weather, you 'gear up and go.' That's our motto. But still, you think about nature's beauty and nature's danger. You give one the love it deserves and the other the respect it demands," Mo replied.

Hours passed as we fished.

* * *

Fog is sneaky. It gradually thickens, leaching away your vision a tiny bit at a time. We spent most of our time looking down at the water, monitoring our lines. Mo scanned the horizon in between rebaits, so assumedly he noticed it first, but he was a native Alaskan, and these sorts of things simply didn't faze him as much as us. The fog was closing us in, like we were a delicate artifact packed in a box stuffed with cotton. The world around us was steadily turning white, and all sounds, even our own, became muffled.

"We're getting socked in, it seems," Avery noted. I could tell there was a tinge of concern in his voice, but we were three men on a fishing trip with a guide twice our age. A certain level of macho bravado was expected.

"Yup," Mo replied, picking something from under one finger nail idly.

"Do we need to head in? Or do use radar or something in fog?" I asked. It must've been obvious to everyone that I was the worrier of the group.

Mo stopped and scanned the water's surface. On one side, where we were closer to shore, a dark mass could still be seen behind the damp white wall, indicating where the mountains were. "No radar. We can go, if you want." Then Mo decided to tell us a story. "I knew a guy from not too far away, was fishing in these waters one time when fog came in strong."

"What happened to him?" I asked.

"He was socked in. Couldn't see ten feet off the bow. Figured he could get over near the shore, follow that home. But it's pretty uneven. And even a dozen feet off shore, the depth's probably twenty-five feet or more. Anyway, he started back that way, keeping the shore on his left. Didn't see the rocks until he hit them. Even at a low speed, boats don't like hitting things or getting hit by things."

I gave a look around at the fog closing us in, imaging a similar fate. "Oh man, did he make it back?"

"Yeah, yeah." My tensed shoulders dropped, relieved. "Managed to guide the sinking boat to shore, or close enough near, then he hiked back. The land's as unforgiving as the sea. Took him three days, as I recall." Suddenly, my concern grew exponentially. Three days? I wasn't sure what I'd do, or if I'd be able to survive. I didn't want to find out, either. I really wanted to get back to the lodge.

Dave gave me a look, realizing my concern. I just wish Dave hadn't been such a helper. Why couldn't he just let the captain do the captain's work?

"Yeah, why don't we head in? Can't hardly see land now," he said with a gesture toward the far off, disappearing shore. "I can raise the anchor," Dave said.

Mo nodded, with eyebrows raised. "I won't turn the offer down." Dave stepped out of the walled cockpit and walked up to the bow to pull in the anchor. Mo started the engine, then slowly guided the boat away from shore to give slack to the anchor line. After a little maneuver, Dave began to haul up the line, but with more than 300 feet to bring up, we knew it'd take a while. The rattling sound of the chain made a rhythmic *crunk*... pause... *crunk*... pause... as Dave hauled it up a bit at a time.

Behind that sound and mostly masked by it, I began to hear a low rumble, off to my right, some distance away.

"You hear that?" Avery asked, quizzically. When I nodded to confirm, I noticed Avery was looking off the other side of the boat. Straining in that direction, I realized a similar sound was coming from that side as well.

"Mo — what's that sound?" The captain had been distracted, watching Dave with the anchor line.

"Sound?" he asked, confused. Avery and I pointed off both sides of the boat.

"Yeah, a mechanical sort of rumble, on both sides of us," Avery said.

A moment passed before all hell broke loose.

* * *

Commercial fishing boats sometimes use a process called pair trawling. The concept is simple: two boats, with their combined engine power and size, can drag a huge net through the water between their vessels and collect a massive catch. Plus, the sound of each boat's engine drives the fish away from the boat but often into the net.

And although we were technically inside the Department of Fish and Game markers, meaning no commercial boats should've been fishing there, people make mistakes. And sometimes people fudge the rules.

They'd probably done it dozens of times before. After all, we were in an incredibly remote place. The likelihood that they'd be seen or caught was virtually zero. If they were trawling inside the markers on purpose, I'm sure the two boat captains thought to themselves that another half mile inland wouldn't kill anyone.

They were wrong.

* * *

Mo popped up from his captain's chair with suddenness and urgency. "Get that anchor up!" he shouted to Dave, who was already hauling as fast as he could. Avery and I looked to each other in confusion. Then we heard a new sound. A growing whoosh across the water. The boat began a gentle turn as Dave continued to haul in the chain, now trying doubly hard at Mo's urging.

The captain was halfway between cockpit and bow when we were hit.

Something slammed into the boat from under the water and set us moving, fast, as if a giant had come up beneath us and the reached out to take us away. Avery and I fell to the floor of the cockpit. I saw Mo flip overboard. Though I didn't hear him hit the water, my first thoughts were of the certain death that awaited him there.

Surely Dave dropped the anchor line, I thought. Surely that would stop us.

I realized afterward that we had been swept up by the net of the two fishing boats that went past us on either side. Though our craft was not large in terms of boats, it was significantly larger than anything any commercial fisherman was expecting to catch in these waters, and with the added drag of our sinking anchor, we must've surprised them on their boats nearly as much as they surprised us.

Bells of alarm rang out on both sides, buried in fog, as the fishing boats warning each other of trouble. To slow down, to turn in. Our boat slowed as this happened, riding a last swell and then coming to a halt on the swaying backs of the waves. Avery and I stood up, looking to the bow for some sign of Dave or the captain, but there were none. Then a shout, from the side nearest Avery.

"It's Mo! In the water!" Avery said.

"We've gotta get him out now or he's dead," I replied, grabbing for the flotation ring that hung next to the captain's chair. At the gunwale, I saw Mo and it was clear he was already in very bad shape. He struggled to call to us, to say anything, while his body curled into a near fetal position. I threw the ring and it landed next to him, but he couldn't grab it. His body had already given up. "Crap, we need to hook him or something!" I tore through the small interior hold and found a boat hook, then rushed back to the edge. Mo was just barely close enough to reach. I hooked his yellow rubber hood and pulled, hard.

As Mo floated back toward the boat, Avery hung dangerously out over the water, but was able to grab the captain. I still have no idea how we did it, but using our combined strength and sheer adrenalin, we dragged Mo clumsily back into the cockpit. He was blue.

As soon as Mo hit the deck, I said, "Cover him. Try to get him warm. I need to look for Dave." I rushed to the bow.

If I live a thousand years, which seems unlikely now, I'll never forget what I saw.

Dave. My friend, Dave. His body, limp and lifeless, floating away on the icy swells. Face down in the water. My mind raced, but how long had it been? A minute? Two? Our momentum had left him far behind, perhaps 40 yards away. Barely breaking the surface, already fading into the white curtain of fog. Making no attempt to swim or pull his face out of the water. My friend Dave was dead.

I heard a loud double-thump as I fell down to the deck. My knees hurt, abstractly. Some time passed, I don't know how much. Then a hand grabbed my shoulder. It was Avery.

"Get up. Come back. I need your help." His eyes were locked on Dave, too, but he managed to keep moving. I didn't budge. Then his hand shook me, hard. Avery's eyes appeared before me, open wide. "Gary. I need you to snap out of it. If you don't, we may all die here, not just Dave." I managed a slight nod.

Around us, somewhere in the murk, the bells continued to clang, getting closer. I heard voices, shouting, engines dropping into gear.

Next thing I knew, I was back in the cockpit, pushed there by momentum or will, and saw that Avery had helped Mo get in new clothes that weren't wet. I dimly imagined that Mo must've kept an extra set around for a rainy day. Well, it was raining hard on this day, I supposed.

We sat in the cockpit for a moment, but Avery couldn't be quiet anymore. "What the hell just happened?" he asked.

"Tallers," Mo said in a slow, forced voice, until suddenly his entire body shook with uncontrolled shivers. He tried to speak again. "Tall. Ink. Lie." He sat in the captain's seat, hunched over before the wheel. The boat's low rumbling engine still hummed in neutral.

"What, Mo? I can't understand you," Avery said, draping Mo's rubber coat over him for another layer of insulation.

Mo struggled to stop the shivers. Only his eyes seemed to be under his control, and they looked around wide and frantic. It was as if he was trying to point with his eyes, left and right. "Tallers," he mumbled again, then made an angry grimace. "Trawlers," he said, through clenched teeth, gasping from the effort once he spit out the word.

"Trawlers," I repeated, considering. "More than one." I rolled my eyes, getting the point. "That's why the sound came from both sides."

Avery snapped his fingers. "I've seen that! On TV, when they drag the net between two boats?" Mo nodded stiffly in response. "Damn. They never saw us. Ran right through us."

Mo made an angry face again. "Not. Here." He tilted his head, slightly. "Not loud."

"He means they're shouldn't be here. They're not *allowed*," I said to

Avery. "We were anchored inside the markers."

Out of the gloom, a dark form materialized off one side of our boat. A loud rumbling shape. The bells were upon us, the shouting, the first of the fishing vessels found us and rolled in close enough to see. New shouts went up, many angry.

From the other side, a second ship emerged from the fog, slowing to position itself opposite the first. We were sandwiched between the much larger fishing boats, one coming to a stop in front of our bow, the other behind our stern. On both, men rushed across the decks.

I noticed Mo, just for a moment, fidgeting in his chair. He shivered and flexed his hand into a harsh fist.

As the boats calmed their commotion, an electronic scratching static sound briefly deafened us. It went silent, then came again, slightly less loud. A speaker of some kind.

"Fishing vessel!" the call came out, in a thick accent I didn't recognize. "Do you require aid?"

I looked at Avery, exhausted, dumbfound. Did we need aid? Nothing would bring back Dave now. But did Mo need help? Absolutely.

Avery nodded slightly, a look that was anger and fear and sadness, deciding to be our voice. "Our friend," Avery paused, looking down, his voice breaking. "He was knocked overboard. When your... line or net or... whatever... hit us."

There was an extended silence, the only sound being the low rumble of our engine and the calm lapping of the water on the ships' hulls.

The speaker crackled. "But he is okay? Have you given him new clothes and warmth?" Behind us, Mo uttered a gurgling sound, strangely animal.

Avery proceeded, sharply shaking his head. "This man," he said, pointing toward Mo, "needs additional aid. But another man, our friend... Dave... was lost, overboard."

For another long moment, the speaker was silent. On the deck, the men of the commercial fishing boats passed comments to each other, unheard by us. Finally the speaker crackled again. "You have our deepest sympathies for your loss from this tragic accident. We did not anticipate your craft in the waters marked for fishing."

Mo spat, huffing out air. "Inside!" he breathed. Every word, every thought seemed a struggle for him. Like breaking through his own fog. Mo's face was down, looking at the steering wheel and the boat's controls.

Avery's brow furrowed. He shouted a response. "But we weren't outside the markers! We—"

Suddenly, the boat lurched forward, causing both Avery and me to tumble to the deck again. Looking up, I saw Mo, still hunched over the wheel, with one hand on the throttle, jammed fully forward. The noise of the engine erupted in our ears, but only for a couple of seconds.

Then the only sounds were metal and wood and tearing and shouting. We were thrust into the forward section of the cockpit as the boat abruptly stopped. Heavy things splashed into the water. I could see one of the fishing boats looming over us, above us even, far too close.

With a deliberate, jerky action, Mo pulled the throttle back, and our boat separated from the fishing boat. I heard frantic yelling in another language, but had no idea what they said. Standing, I saw a ragged hole in the side of the fishing vessel. Mo had rammed the ship. Our metal boat seemed intact, but the ship in front of us was listing, taking on water. I saw several men floating beside the boat, their movements quickly diminishing.

Then, with another grunt of effort, Mo thrust the boat forward, turning the wheel and sending us blindly into the fog.

* * *

"What the hell are you doing?" Avery raged, grasping Mo's shoulders. Avery was much younger, much bigger, much stronger. As our boat buzzed through the blanket of fog, Avery swiveled Mo in the captain's seat so they could be eye to eye.

Mo looked like a man near death, most certainly deranged. The experience in the water had done something, something very bad, to him. He mouthed words, but only grunts and sounds came out.

Frustrated, Avery let the chair spin back, then reached for the throttle to stop the boat. I heard Avery cough.

Then Mo was covered in a spray of blood, blinking.

Avery fell to the deck with a terrifying, gurgling sound that didn't come from his mouth. It bubbled out of the gaping hole in his throat.

I looked at Avery in shock and alarm, my eyes wide. "What the hell—!" Then I saw the hook in Mo's hand, the one he had used to spike the halibut. He hunched over the wheel, turning the boat slowly. As I realized what he had done, an immense anger grew in me and I rushed toward him. "You son of a bitch!"

That's when he plunged the hook into the right side of my chest and a pain beyond anything I'd ever known consumed me. I fell with the hook still dangling between my ribs.

As I lay on the deck, I looked over at my dying friend, Avery. His eyes were staring, not seeing, and his mouth opened and closed slowly, like a fish out of water. The slash at his neck flowed red and bubbled with his attempts to speak. Above us, Mo lost control of himself and his head fell into the steering wheel with a thump before he was able to push himself up again. He turned the wheel and I heard bells again.

We were approaching the fishing boats again.

There were louder shouts. The men aboard those fishing boats must've heard our engine, knew we were coming back.

Mo had gone crazy. It had to have been the water. The water froze the sanity in Mo and consumed it. Now, he was just a lurching rage.

I had to get up. I had to do something. Though they were responsible for my friend's death, those men on the fishing boats didn't deserve to die. But Mo. He killed Avery in cold blood.

He would have to answer to me.

I bit into my lip, hard, as I pulled the hook out of my body. Still, I gasped. Lying on the deck trying to hide the hook was the worst pain I'd ever known. With a struggle, I turned my head up to sneak a glance at Mo.

His eyes were intent. Looking forward. He held the wheel steady, though his hands shook. He forced his arms to lock, to hold the boat on course.

I worked my way onto my knees. Then, using the gunwale for support, I stood.

In front of us, a shadow loomed in the fog. Bells came from nearby.

Mo fell against the throttle, taking the boat up to its full speed as we raced toward the shadow in the fog. I had to stop him. I raised the hook in my right hand.

And I saw the fishing boats, one high and dry, the other sinking into the frosty water, slide by on our right. Mo seemed not to have seen them. He looked intently forward at the shadow, clenching the wheel.

If not the fishing boats, then what?

Wisps fell away as it came nearer. A giant in front of us. An unbeatable giant. Mo's slow mind realized his error, but it was too late.

As the small aluminum boat crumpled against the unyielding rocky surface of the island, Mo was thrust with deadly force into the steering console and I flew into the hold.

* * *

I awoke. Was it days or hours later? The boat didn't crack and sink, but rather bent and reformed. It was almost a part of the small rocky island now.

Dazed, I stood and went back into the cockpit. Mo sat just where I'd seen him last, though broken. His forehead indented strangely where it struck the wheel. On the deck, Avery was crumpled and lifeless. Spinning slowly, I took in a view that was nothing but white fuzz.

"Hello?" I called, and a searing pain came from my right lung as tears welled to my eyes. "Is anyone out there?"

There was no reply, no sound. The fog removed all sound, and I knew I was utterly alone.

KEITH SOARES

||||| |||||

The Fingers of the Colossus

"What a shit job. Outliers?"

"Pillip, shut it."

"He's right, Colonel. We'll be gone at least two years. For what?"

"Is there still a place for you in Her Royal Arms, Jamerick? Do you obey? Do you still get paid?"

"Don't get offended, sir. I'll do what I am told, but the *people* out there. They're like animals," Jamerick complained.

"Not *like* animals, Jam. They are animals." Cackling at this stupid joke, Pillip was pissing me off. I turned to him.

"Should we discuss *hours*, Major Ragus?" I raised an eyebrow at him. His shoulders slumped, deflated.

"Sir, no, sir. I'm just… just joking. No harm… Colonel…" He was backpedaling, but still not taking me seriously enough.

"We do what we're told, private to general. You have an opinion, then I have a suggestion: tell it to yourself, quietly, in the mirror. Or it's hours we talk." Everyone had heard this little speech of mine before. They knew it meant *no more arguments*.

He saluted. "Sir!" He was mad at me, but I didn't care. He raced off. I turned to Jamerick and tilted my head, and Jam suddenly found somewhere else to be, too. Usually I was close with my senior officers, easy. But I didn't like anyone questioning the command chain. I was in charge. On an Outlier mission, questioning command was a step below mutiny. And I liked my head attached.

Once they cleared out, I looked up at the com port. "Orders." Recognizing my face and voice, com displayed the mission orders in front of me.

Col Smit Jolliam, Mission Commander, IOSec4:

Rendezvous @ 98CFT-01, landing CC001, on SD342 @ 00:01:00IPMT.

Entire Reg. Priority :: A / Secrecy :: 5 / Contingency :: None / Join ::
CargoTrans, SD372

Addl orders forthcoming.

EOT

"Com dismiss." The display disappeared. I already knew what I had to do. And I knew what we were up to. Head to the Outliers, section 4, a planet the locals called *C'Olnus*. That meant *'Land of God'* in direct translation. Bunch of pagan zealot nuts, from what I'd heard. Never mind. My job was just to get there, and obviously in a huge show of force. Entire regiment… I hadn't taken the entire regiment anywhere in some time. We weren't going to be negotiating. *Additional orders forthcoming.* Yeah, something like *take everything and leave them for dead.* Well, we'd done it before. There was always a reason. Her majesty's realm was vast and I was just a small part. We do what we're told, private to general.

"Com lookup: *C'Olnus*." Almost instantly, a view of the planet appeared, with text beside. "Read," I commanded. The com responded in a voice intended to sound like a soothing female. Most people hated the voice. The men called her Irma, or just the Bitch. I personally didn't care one way or the other. She was just part of the job.

"*C'Olnus*: Outlier in section 4, system 98CFT, first planet from the star. Indoctrinated into the realm HMY5642." *Damn, they've been part of the realm for only 2 years. Didn't take them long to piss someone off.* "Inhabitable: Yes. Atmosphere: Partial N—"

"Com skip to inhabitants," I said, absent-mindedly rubbing my left eye. I sat down.

After a moment's pause, it resumed.

"Inhabitants: Pagan tribes comprise the entire population of the planet. Races: four distinct, 27 subclassifications."

"Tell me about CC001." The landing location. Com went quiet, found the data, then spoke again.

"CC001 represents the primary dwelling location of the *Olnipus* tribe, meaning '*People of God*.' This location is called *Jn Q'harus*, '*The Ten Fingers*.' Population: 19,457. Primary dwelling type: primitive construction single-story huts, mud and straw. Diet: The *Olnipus* hunt and eat wild game indigenous to their area, predominantly the *kyva*, a type of deer. In addition, they are avid farmers and eat a wide variety of grains, especially a corn-like grain called *veetha*, as well as other leafy ve—"

"Skip ahead to resource quantities," I said, picking a speck of dirt from under one fingernail. Com obliged and rattled off several figures. Very large figures. "Why the devil do they have so *much* of the stuff?" I asked myself aloud. Com took it as a command.

"Primary use of resources: religious rituals, consump—"

"Com, stop." The less I knew about the people I may have to kill, the better. I prefer a dreamless sleep.

* * *

Central One had always been my home, and by that luck of the draw, I had easy access to the academy, training. There had never been an Outlier subject who'd even made officer, much less colonel. I was the third colonel in three generations of my family.

Sure, the other planets of Central, those nearest to One, had produced plenty of officers, but only from their wealthy families, those able to send their children to One and the academy.

The Outliers were poor. Pagan. Shunned and disrespected. Many times, men, especially new men, would question why the realm even kept Outliers around. The answer was obvious. Not everyone can be queen. Someone's got to clean the lavatories. Or, in the case of the Outliers, provide the things the realm needed but didn't want to get our hands dirty with: food, raw materials, cheap (or free) labor. If you were an Outlier and you had ore, grain, or even just people, you might get a visit from us. We made bad houseguests. But then, it's how the saying goes. *Render unto the Queen that which is the Queen's.* And the Queen owned everything. Even her subjects.

* * *

The carriers were primed. The men were ready. The usual pomp and circumstance of a large away was happening all around, but I had to do it. I leaned over and feigned an itch on my face. To stifle my yawn. Bless the Queen, but this could be tedious. I wanted to be gone. Three full carriers. More than four thousand men per vessel. Twelve thousand under my command. As for firepower, I could carry one of our L-class guns and wipe out the entire planet of *C'Olnus*. I yawned again. I appreciated the Queen's trust in me, but these tasks were so… boring.

We launched on time, in perfect formation, saluting back to the sendoff party as expected, on screen from our bridge. All three carriers on a plane together, aligned left to right. Using standard thrust, we separated and put the regulation safe distance between each of us and One. Any observer on One or any of the three ships would have to use satcom to see the others now. I sat up.

The men, most of whom didn't understand how things worked, typically found the shift boring. I, on the other hand, knew all too well the dangers and paid very close attention. Shifting any ship into superluminal was a risk, to the ship, its crew, and in fact everyone in the vicinity. I leaned toward my display and gave the command. *Go.*

First, carrier *HMRAV Quintero* deployed its nearly-invisible O-ring. There was the normal flash and sluicing effect, then she was gone. Next, *HMRAV Zephyr*. Finally, it was our turn. "Com all ship. *Attention crew of HMRAV Janus I, this is Colonel Jolliam. Prepare for superluminal. Deploy O-ring, on my mark...*" On the bridge, a lieutenant nodded toward me, telling me all was ready. "*Mark.*" I switched off the com and within seconds, we left One behind.

* * *

The men are bored by superluminal because they think it's the same as standard thrust, just a lot faster. It's not. For superluminal, our O-ring literally alters space around our vessel. We aren't propelled, as there is in fact no known means to be propelled in a superluminal manner. Instead, space shifts and we free fall faster than light. Remember that, in space, there is no up or down. But by warping space around us — somewhat like making our own up and down, with down being the direction we want to go — we fall. The number of possible things that can go wrong boggles the mind, ranging from pressures on the ship and crew, to the possible annihilation of our destination. For that reason, our three ships headed to three distinct empty regions of space near our destination, using standard thrust to then complete the journey, much as we did to start it.

But three ships shifting superluminal at the same time presents another problem. We call it *fatal overlap*. Basically, it means that the effects of one ship's O-ring comes too close to another's.

Fifteen years ago, I experienced it first-hand. Sloppy navigating by someone on either the *HMRAV Intelligence*, or the *HMRAV Beacon IV*, led to a fatal overlap. Calling it *fatal* overlap was truly redundant; there was no non-fatal version. Luckily my ship was on the opposite side of an

Outlier planet named *Haccian 3*. When the overlap happened, the planet was between my ship and the explosion, or else I'd be dust. *Haccian 3* lost its atmosphere and more than forty million inhabitants died. Even behind the planet, we were tossed like a child's toy, losing significant outer rigging and suffering one hull breech that was thankfully containable.

After that, people smarter than me took a lot of readings, interviewed me and my crew countless times, did untold calculations, and determined the regulation safe distance. It's what we've followed ever since, and the distance we put between our ships and Central One when we left. I still have no doubt that the Queen hid in her protective bunker whenever there'd be a shift anywhere near her planet. Given what I saw happen, I'm rather surprised she let shifts happen nearby in the first place.

* * *

By Her Grace, the fall went well. Long and boring and by the book. The worst thing to happen was reprimanding four men for gambling in the shared quarters. A stupid offense to take an official warning for, considering everyone did it, even the officers. You had to be lazy and dimwitted not to understand the simple unwritten rules all the men used to hide the offense. Still, there was much worse that could happen, so I was pleased with the fall. We dropped out of superluminal on target and retracted the O-ring. Waiting by within scanner distance were *Quintero* and *Zephyr*. That, too, was a relief. In superluminal, there was no way to communicate, no way to send or receive warning. We sent the supposedly less important ships first, to lead the way or act as scouts, but even if they dropped into the middle of Armageddon, we'd never know until we got there. We pulled in formation and ran under standard toward the planet.

For just a moment or two, I tried to imagine what they saw. Pagans, hut-dwellers. They probably didn't even know they were part of the realm. All that mattered to us was that they were ours, not a place contested by some other rulers of the galaxy. We slid into orbit. From the surface, they must've seen three mysterious new stars, bright, oddly oblong discs, now arranged in a triangle. Truth be told, it was another of our tactics with the pagans — fear of God (or Gods, or whatever else they might worship). We control the sky.

With a low tone, com notified me of new orders. They were basically what I expected. Generous even. The good news was this should be a relatively short visit. Out of habit, I asked com a question I always asked after a fall. "Success estimate?"

Com replied. "96%." It was the expected answer. Some mathematician, I have no idea who, decided that *all* missions began with a 4% chance of failure. So we were no worse than average, in the eyes of com. I turned my attention back to the duties at hand.

Protocol demanded that the initial landing party be six, each carrying L-class guns. In addition, four of the six were to be heavily armed Gunners, loaded with A-class. The remaining two were our emissaries, expected to be Major Ragus, and Jam — Lieutenant Colonel Pehk Jamerick. But I was bored from the drop. I didn't want to sit up on *Janus I* and wait while they did everything. So I pulled rank and joined the party. That really ticked off Jam, as he was now senior on deck, had to stay with the ship. He got to be bored instead of me. Little did we know his boredom wouldn't last. The other two carriers each sent their own landing craft. Eighteen of us, total. More than enough men and firepower to handle twenty thousand or so pagans.

Nearly five months after we set out from One, we approached our landing at CC001, the place the locals called *The Ten Fingers... Jn Q'harus*. As we entered the atmosphere, it was clear why. On a high bluff, overlooking their large village, spikes of stone jutted into the sky, brown and solid, making a curving arc of vertical shafts. They weren't perfect cylinders, more like irregular stone monoliths sticking up from the stony ground. Sure enough, there were ten. Behind the bluff, the ground fell away into a deep, nearly circular depression, echoing the curve of the ten rock fingers.

By protocol, we did three flyovers, noisy and low, to get their attention, then we landed on the opposite side of the village from the *Fingers*, in the lowlands, flat territory, among the endless golden fields. On the last approach, we nearly brushed two of the *Fingers*. That *really* got their attention. Skimming the bluff, I gauged that each of our landing craft was about half as long as the run of the stony outcroppings. A single *Finger* was more than ten times the size of one of the humanoid natives running out to see what was happening. Scores of them were present when we landed and stepped out.

With one look, I was pretty sure we were their first. *Shit*. Typically, on a first visit with a pagan race, we were considered gods. It could be useful in getting anything you wanted from the locals, but generally it just meant they wouldn't leave you alone. Of course, we could always switch to the 'vengeful god' routine, too.

As they approached, we stood in a V formation, with me at the front, Pillip slightly behind and to my left, the four Gunners arrayed two per side. The other two landing parties made similar Vs to our left and right, but a bit behind. Everyone deferred to me as mission commander. Every man wore a translator, a nearly invisible bud in one ear connected to a small arc of clear material. The translators allowed us to hear everything the natives said, rendered in the Queen's Speech, and they broadcast our words in the local language. But translators didn't replace the original speech, they just added to it. It made for an odd effect. When the native's spoke, we heard them privately in our own language, on the bud in our ear. But when we spoke, they could hear us, simultaneously, in both the Queen's Speech and their tongue. Typically, this odd duality just increased the locals' impression of us as gods.

I stood, waiting for someone to approach. Looking superior. Feeling superior. For honestly, wasn't I? The ground rumbled slightly, shaking the landscape. In my ear, com reported. "Minor tremor. No expected damages." I rolled my eyes, annoyed at such trivialities. Finally, one of their numbers stepped forward, a short, plump woman, with silver hair. She began speaking in her own tongue, converted into recognizable speech for our ears by our translators.

"You are from the new stars," she said, pointing skyward. It wasn't even a question. "Why have you come here?" For a moment, I was taken aback. No reverence, no bowing, no flowery words of praise. It was the first hint I had that told me this mission would be much different than I anticipated. Than anyone anticipated.

"Have you…" I said slowly, even stammering a bit. "Have you seen such stars before?"

She didn't hesitate. "We have seen them, yes. From other worlds." *Well, not their first visit, then.*

"Yes," I said, regaining my full composure and air of superiority. "Yes. We are from another world. In fact, we are from the world that *rules* all worlds. It is called Central One." Many cowered at the name, which was not translated at all. It came out of my mouth and the translator the same way, amplifying the words to great effect. *So, they've heard of Central. Why wasn't this in the brief?*

"Why have you come?" she asked. *Blunt. Okay, I could be blunt.*

"In 30 of my world's days — that is, approximately 22 of your days — a large vessel from our world will land here." I gestured to the flatlands around us. "At that time, you are required to harvest all of these fields and provide the bounty to your Queen, who has sent us for this purpose. This includes — " and here no translation would suffice, so I pronounced their words as best I could, though honestly I didn't care much if I misspoke " — *d'san, panoci, f'bref,* and *veetha.*" As the last word came out, a tremendous gasp escaped the lips of the pagan crowd. I continued. "But your Queen is not unjust. We shall leave behind 10 percent of the yield, that you may be rewarded for your contribution to the realm." I stood calmly before them, brooking no argument or compromise.

A hush fell. Then the woman spoke again. She shook her head, and made a peculiar downward gesture with two fingers of her right hand. "It is not possible," she said, spitting.

I puffed myself up. The men around me adjusted their weapons in a thinly veiled threat. After a deliberate pause, I replied. "It *will* be done."

She repeated. "It is not possible. *Without life, there is no life.*" It sounded she was like quoting some pagan religious text.

I didn't become mission commander and have an entire regiment at my disposal because I was easy to get along with. I turned to one of the Gunners and nodded, and he lowered his weapon at the old woman. A second gasp went up from the crowd.

I took a step back toward her and peered down into her eyes that were clouding with age. Once I knew I had her attention, I gave the old woman an uncaring sneer. "*It will be done.*" She cowered below me and looked aside. It was as if she was ignoring me, ignoring the gun pointed at her, but contemplating a somehow worse fate. After a moment, I stood straight and proper, turned and resumed my position at the head of our V formation. I looked over the crowd of natives with disdain, and said in a loud voice, "Her Majesty has been kind in choosing to leave you with enough food to survive. Do not disrespect this gift again." The silent populace just stared. So, I nodded and turned to leave. That was enough for day one.

Behind me, the old crone spoke again, louder, with a passion that was part anger, part fear. "*It is not possible! Without life, there is no life!*" she cried at my back. I froze, standing stiffly erect, annoyed. I turned my head sideways to the nearest Gunner.

"Give them an example," I commanded. He nodded in response.

As I walked back toward the landing craft, I heard the wails and uproar of the pagans as the Gunner followed his orders. Under our feet, the ground made a brief deep rumble.

* * *

We stayed at CC001, aboard our landing crafts, biding our time. There was no concern of attack or retribution for the death of their leader; the automated defenses of our small ships were sufficient to kill every native on the planet.

I had the intention to let them wait, then to speak to whatever next leader they might have and force the issue. I knew we needed their submission, if only because there was no way my men — my *trained* men — were going to harvest crops for these people. If not the second leader, then the third, or the fourth. One of them would listen and the people would do what was required. But time was finite. In no way would I allow the crops to wither in the fields. There would be action, and soon.

On two of our idle days, we experienced light tremors. After the second, and in the privacy of my quarters, I queried com. "Historical record on planet seismology."

"No direct data. Remote observations indicate occasional light activity."

"Success estimate?"

"94%."

Good.

* * *

After eight of their days, a much younger woman stood alone outside my vessel, waiting for acknowledgement. *Even their young are brash and disrespectful.* I looked up from the reading I'd been doing and waved a hand to one of the warrant officers, pointing toward her image on my screen. "Find out what she wants." *If it isn't the answer I require, it may be time to start making myself more clear to these people.*

A moment later, com reported movement outside the craft. A lot of movement. I checked the screens and a slow smile spread across my face.

The warrant officer returned, offering a salute. "Sir, she says they must perform the harvest now."

"Indeed they must. Good," I said. I nodded curtly toward the warrant officer, but he didn't leave. "Is there something else?"

"Sir, she... she said it again. *Without life, there is no life.*"

"So?"

"Well, sir, she said it in a strange way. Like it should mean something to me. To us." He seemed nervous. God, I hated nervous junior officers around me. I waved him out.

What the devil is with these people? I mused a moment, then consulted com. "Look up phrase 'Without life, there is no life' in the local language." A moment passed and the answer, as it were, was given.

"Insufficient explanation. In the language of the *Olnipus*, the phrase is spoken often, as a reverent chant or mantra." *You've got that correct*, I thought, rolling my eyes. "The term for 'life' is *veetha*, however, the tribe's primary crop is also called *veetha,* a corn-like grain grown in great quantities on the planet. It is unclear, due to lack of records from their culture, whether *veetha* in the phrase is referring to 'life,' the grain, or both." Com went silent.

Odd bastards. Without life, there is no life. Without grain, there is no life. Without life, there is no grain. Without grain, there is no grain.

I sighed, audibly, and rubbed the bridge of my nose. But the answer was obvious. The tribe considered the grain crops to be so fundamental to their ability to live, that they had used the same term for both things. *Veetha* was their crop. *Veetha* was their life.

"And we're here to take it away…" I thought aloud.

"Correct. Current orders instruct this regiment to—"

"Com, silent." *I know what my orders are. To hell with them all. We've come for your crops. Your* veetha. *If that means also taking your 'life,' well, then...* I shrugged, giving a little smirk. Orders were orders, and I was very good at ensuring they were followed.

* * *

So they harvested. And harvested. The grain, of a number of types but clearly dominated by the corn-like *veetha*, was stored in a large cave at the base of the nearby rocky hills. The same hills that led up the *Fingers*. I was told they kept the harvest in the cave to keep it cool, to avoid spoilage. To be certain of this, I had my men investigate. The *veetha* — and the rest of it, whatever all that was called — was the Queen's property now, after all. The men reported back that the cave was, remarkably, providing a safe and evenly cooled storehouse, and that incredibly little of the grain was being lost to rot or vermin. The *Olnipus* were diligent about keeping their harvest safe. At least one could respect them for that, and I was glad not to have to order the stuff moved. Providing storage space for it would've required a lot of trips to the carrier group — first to haul it all up there, second to haul it all back and put it aboard the freighter ship, once that hulking beast arrived. I preferred my men doing more civilized tasks.

For twelve days, they harvested. On occasion, tremors shook the ground, but the natives hardly noticed. Finally the job was done. I was tired just watching them. Waiting aboard the landing craft was a far cry from the comforts of the carrier. My quarters, comparatively, were cramped, and I began to wish I had let Jam lead the away team after all. Pillip was just as restless as I, but more vocal about it. Wedged into my small quarters one evening, we watched on our screens as the locals filtered out of the fields and headed back to their village for the night. Pillip sipped on a steaming cup of tea.

Calmly, he spoke. "I told you this was a shit job."

I nodded. "Yes, I know."

"Two days?"

"Yes." We both knew the answer already. Pillip just asked to pass the time. The freighter was due soon.

"How many to get it loaded, for us to get out of here?" He paused over his tea briefly, eyes locked on me.

I looked up from the screen, double-checking quick calculations in my head. I had already made the estimate to myself a dozen times. "No more than three days once the freighter lands. We'll impress upon the locals the importance of speed." I smirked and Pillip huffed with his own smug smile. He took another sip of tea.

Com toned, not loud, but a low note that immediately made us sit up.

Alarm.

"Incoming urgent message," com announced.

"Accept," I replied. On screen, a corporal I didn't recognize appeared. *A corporal, calling me directly. Better be good, son.*

"Sir," he began breathlessly, "apologies for the interruption. But the grain. It's not in the cave." He panted several times, wearing a concerned look like he didn't know which was worse, the news or my potential reaction.

"Then *where is it*, corporal?" I leaned toward the screen.

"Sir, we don't know. It's just gone."

For a moment, I sat frozen. *Gone? What the devil were these pagans up to?* I looked calmly at the screen. "Protocol 682, corporal. *Find that damned stuff now.* Out." I slammed a fist onto the desk as com disconnected the conversation.

Pillip had already leaped out of his chair and was now standing next to me. "How's this possible?"

My eyes bored holes in the dark screen in front of me, as I stared at my own angry reflection. "I don't know. Yet. But I do know that these pagan scum are about to get a very stern lesson in respect."

* * *

A short time later, Pillip and I walked into the mostly empty cave. My men were everywhere, scouring the place for information. Others patrolled the village and surrounding area, and two of the landing craft were in the air, all scanners wide open.

Seeing us, Chief Warrant Officer Makio quickly strode in our direction. "Sir, the platforms are gone as well, they must've rolled them out. That's how they moved everything so fast — in between night watch shifts."

"Rolled them out *where?*" Pillip asked. I raised my right hand slightly.

This was my show. I nodded for the officer to continue.

"There's a way out in the back. We didn't know about it before."

I lifted an eyebrow. "Who was in charge of investigating the cave, *Chief Warrant Officer Makio?*"

"Me, sir," he said, hardly concealing a thick gulping swallow.

"That may prove a very costly oversight." At that moment, com toned in my earpiece and I tapped to accept. Lieutenant Colonel Ambrank, of the *Quintero*'s landing craft, gave a hasty report.

"We've found it, sir. A caravan headed up the bluff."

"Good. We're on our way to you. Stop them, but do nothing else until we arrive. Out."

"Yes, sir."

I turned to leave the cave, knowing Makio would be relieved that the heat of my focused attention would soon be on someone else.

* * *

We found them near the top of the bluff, under the looming pillars of the *Fingers*. I conferred briefly with Ambrank, who told me that the locals were adamant about proceeding. His men were forced to kill two of the natives who wouldn't otherwise respond to their demands to stop. We looked over a group of pagans who trembled in fear.

But it was strange…

Their fear did not seem to be directed at *us*. They kept looking away, up the hill.

"Turn this caravan around. Take the harvest back to the cave. Now." There were dozens of the biggest men from the tribe holding ropes that attached to carts holding the grain, surrounded by many others from the village.

"We cannot." It was the same young woman who had approached my landing craft.

"You can and you will, or your people will die here," I replied. This had gone on too long.

"*Without life, there is no life,*" she said again.

I sighed. "Yes, so you have said. Regardless, turn this caravan around."

"We cannot," she replied solemnly, eyes flitting to the *Fingers* above us.

I turned to a nearby Gunner and nodded. Randomly, he cut down three of the men pulling carts. The others made a collective anguished cry. I looked back at the woman. She remained resolute, but some behind her started to look aside. *So... not everyone is as zealous as this one*, I thought. I considered having the Gunner take out another few natives.

Before I could give the command, all hell broke loose.

The ground below us shook violently, at the same moment when dozens of villagers arrived in support of their kind. They streamed over the nearby hills and toward my men. By protocol, we fired, tearing through them and piling up casualties. Still, they were many. They rushed toward us. I watched as several of my men were overcome, killed with blunt instruments like crude clubs and axes.

A circle formed around me and the other officers and we backed toward Ambrank's craft waiting behind us. "Protect the harvest. Close formation." The men, my well-trained men, instantly leaped to follow orders. The natives died in droves. But they kept coming, dozens becoming a hundred, then more. My men gunned them down with no more effort than it took to pass the time.

To pass the time.

To *waste* our time. It was a decoy.

Several of the carts had moved, reaching the top of the bluff, cresting the hill between two of the stone *Fingers*. There, the young woman, that brash young woman who dared confront me, guided her people as they began to overturn the carts.

"Lieutenant Colonel Ambrank. We have a major problem," I said pointing upward. "That is your Queen's property, and it is being destroyed." Ambrank curtly nodded and rushed aboard his landing craft, as I followed.

Without prompting, com spoke in my ear. "Success estimate: 78%." I scowled. *The devil take these bastards.*

"Major Ragus!" Pillip stepped in front of me and saluted crisply. "Finish this group off, then take a team to the village. Leave no one alive." He hurried off without a word.

As I stepped aboard Ambrank's ship, its hatch was sealed. Moments later, the ship leaped off the rocky ground and spun to face uphill. As we passed over the crest of the bluff and past the *Fingers*, I saw what the *Olnipus* tribe was doing.

They were throwing the grain, full cartloads of the stuff, into that gaping maw of a hole on the backside of the bluff, the one I'd seen during our flyovers when we first arrived. The hole seemed to drop forever, the grain falling away into the darkness of the deep. Far, far below, a dull reddish glow lit the pit, the molten innards of the world.

Wasting my *grain for some absurd pagan ritual.* Wordlessly, I nodded toward Ambrank, and he unleashed the full power of the landing craft's weapons upon them. They died, some where they stood, other tumbling off to follow the harvest into the great chasm.

In moments, it was over. But not before two of the carts had been emptied into the hole. The pagans continued their ritual even as they were cut apart.

Tossing the grain, the *veetha*, their life, into a deep hole like they were giving it back to the earth. Like they were feeding the earth.

One way or another, I was going to leave the planet with the rest of the grain. My men dragged the carts back down the bluff and into the cave, as we awaited the arrival of the freighter.

Over the next two days, deep vibrations shook the landscape, like echoes of thunder bubbling underground.

* * *

On schedule, the freighter arrived. The *Olnipus* were now a tribe in the historical record only. But there would be no fear of losing this planet's crops in future years: plenty of Her Majesty's subjects on planets closer to One needed work. By the time of the next planting, the world of the *Olnipus* would be a distant memory as a new race would take over this land and its crops.

As if punctuating the arrival, the ground shook fiercely while the freighter touched down next to my landing craft. It was a huge thing, dwarfing my vessel, though of course nowhere near the size of my carrier orbiting above.

I met with the freighter's commanding officer, so far below me in the chain of command that I didn't bother catching his name, and told him to load the ship as quickly as possible. With no locals to do the work, he sheepishly requested assistance, and out of desire to be away from this hellish place, I permitted one thousand of my lowest ranking men to assist.

Over three days, the ship was loaded. The rumbling earth became a constant, no longer a random series of tremors, but instead a deep background note and constant shaking movement, like we were aboard a huge ship with the engine throbbing.

The freighter was nearly loaded when the devil himself broke loose of hell and paid us a visit.

* * *

The ground didn't simply shake, it danced. Our landing crafts, reflexively, took to the air to avoid being overturned. Those men who remained on the ground were tossed about like children's toys.

Above us, on the bluff, the *Fingers* broke, folding into the earth like they were curling downward. The stony hillside caved inward with a force that felt equal to our superluminal falls.

"Com, what the devil is going on?" I shouted.

"Major seismic event, presenting significant risk to ships, crew, and mission. Recommend abort."

On the deck of my ship, I slammed the console. *Damn it!* Mission failure? On *my résumé*? Impossible. Punching a button, I hailed the freighter. "Commander. *Get as much of that grain as you can without risking the ship, then get your ass into orbit. Now. We're leaving.*" I punched the button again to terminate the transmission before he could respond. Tapping another command into com, I reached out to Jamerick on my carrier. "Jam. This place is falling apart. We're taking what we can, then we'll meet you. I need you to lead the carriers as low as possible so we can make this quick." He nodded and I broke the connection, the screen going dark.

Damned Outliers. Damned pagans and their damned planets. I fumed.

The men rushed to get the grain aboard the freighter. It was a sloppy and haphazard effort, but most of the harvest was saved. Our three landing craft were loaded and lifted off, in formation around the rising freighter. Jam and the carrier group descended. In moments, we'd be docking, and then we'd leave this hellish world behind for good.

As I turned to give the landscape a last, hateful look, the bluff behind us fell away in a confusion of smoke and debris. A deep and wailing sound accompanied the collapse, like the world was screaming for vengeance. And amid the dark billows of smoke, a shadow arose. A vision. A nightmare.

Its head lifted above the clouds like the rock itself had come alive, massive formations of the hard earth packed together in the form of a lumpy face so massive that it alone dwarfed my ship. And it opened its

125

huge, gaping mouth. There, inside, a deep and familiar reddish glow emanated outward. *Is that…? The glow from the pit? How?*

Still it rose, higher, ever higher. Already the stony beast's giant shoulders and chest were above us. And yet it continued to rise.

The dust and smoke simultaneously rose with it, while falling off of it in waves. Below, in the lowlands of the village, nothing could be seen, as the spreading cloud obscured the world.

I ordered our formation to rise quickly, but the monster was faster, much higher than us. It stepped toward us, leaving the rubble of the hills behind.

And there, standing before us was a colossus, a stone golem of immense proportions. Its eyes seemed blind, formations of solid rock incapable of sight. Yet they locked on to us. The thing stepped forward again. It dwarfed the bluff, the village, our landing craft. Had the carriers been near, I dare say this beast would've dwarfed them as well.

The carriers.

Above us, in rapid descent, the three carriers approached, trying to meet up with us as quickly as possible. I have no idea if the beast heard them, saw them, or merely sensed them. But it pulled itself inward, crouching ever so slightly, in a rigid way, its body incapable of true flexibility.

Then, without warning, it leaped into the air with a shuddering force that knocked our craft around like toys, even though we were well off the ground.

On our screens, the colossus was gone.

"Com, align. Where is it?" The view changed.

Above us, climbing impossibly upward, the giant monster was fading like a rocket into the sky… directly toward the approaching shapes of the three carriers. There wasn't even time or a need for my warning. Either their own sensors and alarms would suffice, or they would not.

* * *

I knew them by sight, by the formation they held until the last moment. *Quintero, Zephyr,* and my own *Janus I.*

The colossus, impossibly, had launched itself to their altitude. For a moment, I allowed myself a small smile as *Zephyr* took the vanguard. *Quintero* moved to a flanking position as *Janus I* faded behind. Protect the command vessel. Good.

But in only seconds, my smile faded as *Zephyr* was annihilated. The giant stone monster, using its remaining momentum, smashed into the carrier. It tore through all shields, then through the hull itself. Even from the ground, I could see two distinct portions of *Zephyr* separating. Those men were lost.

I was momentarily blinded as *Quintero* and *Janus I* fired. The beast must have used the husk of *Zephyr,* one of its two divided parts, as both a resting point and launch pad. Taking only a moment to decide, it leaped toward *Quintero.*

Having seen the thing's destructive force, *Quintero* fired as it tried to speed away. Somehow the creature both avoided the attack and made the distance. *Quintero,* like *Zephyr,* was ripped apart.

My shock was tempered by my natural discipline, my inclination to fall back on structure and ingrained tactics. I saw *Janus I* quickly pulling away.

Go superluminal. Damn that colossus and damn us, too. Do it, I thought.

She tried.

* * *

We left the landing crafts behind. They were only useful between orbit and the surface. They would provide no escape. Quickly, we disembarked and rushed aboard the freighter.

Above us, *Janus I* fought valiantly.

How does a thing made of stone do such a thing? How is it alive? Kill the bastard, Jam. When we arrived at this damned planet, I left Lieutenant Colonel Jamerick, my friend, behind. And now he was our only hope of escape. Of making something out of this disaster of a mission.

On *Janus I*, Jam fought the thing, trying to remain at a distance. The colossus jumped between the broken pieces of the other two carriers, seeking a way to get to the last one, as it fired and dodged.

I knew we had to get the freighter into space, go superluminal, get home. If we rescued one vehicle and the grain — that may even be considered heroic. If Jam got home, too, maybe we'd both be awarded medals. Or maybe we'd both be court martialed. But it was my only shot to save my career.

I directed the freighter's captain, but, not knowing the ship, let him remain in command. We rose, then skimmed the landscape, seeking to put distance between us and the fight.

Using the ship's sensors, I could see more clearly what Jam was up against. He did his best. The carrier, a vehicle capable of destroying entire civilizations, possibly entire worlds, fired again and again. It made countless direct hits on the giant stone creature, but its attacks were as effective as firing at the dirt. Burns and flares of char covered the monster, but it was otherwise mostly unhindered. At one moment, we cheered in triumph as *Janus I*'s guns severed one of the thing's hands. The colossus itself continued to fight, as the remainder of its hand and fingers rained to the planet below.

* * *

We raced across the surface of the planet, staying low. Finally, when I felt we had traversed enough distance, I nodded to the captain. "Take her up." He stiffly bowed in response. I was sure that having a Colonel on his ship was not only an alien experience, but also the last thing this captain wanted. We rose.

Alarms went off, several at once. The captain began to sweat, but he commanded by the book. Quadrants checked in, teams were dispatched. Something had happened, but no one was exactly sure what. There was a hull breech, but it was repaired. We continued around the planet, away from the conflict, preparing to leave.

Finally, we were ready. The captain looked at me, like a dog awaiting permission to eat his dinner. "Sir, are we ready for superluminal?" I stood.

"Captain, this is your ship, is it not? I would no more be able to tell you if it is prepared for superluminal than I would tell you if you had wiped your own arse after your last visit to the privy. Get this ship ready, then get us away from this goddamned planet, *now*."

The captain melted before me, but made several commands. The ship's o-rings were deployed.

In short order, we entered the fall. I never saw the colossus, or Jam, or my *Janus I*, again.

* * *

I sat in my quarters on the freighter.

Actually, I used the captain's quarters. I had commandeered them, as ranking officer. We were returning to One, returning with the grain that was so important to someone. At least that part of our mission had succeeded. We'd lost three carriers, but the commanding officer and the grain were returning. In my head, I played out scenarios, seeking to direct blame. I didn't want to simply salvage my career. I wanted to *improve* it.

The fall was a quiet one. I took to reading, and finished a book that I had been slowly attempting to complete for some time. As I flipped the book closed, I felt a familiar sense of satisfaction. Yes, certainly, the mission was flawed. Yes, I had lost three carriers. But I had salvaged the grain, and identified a significant threat to the monarchy.

I was dictating a report to com when a new alarm sounded.

In the hold, amid the huge piles of grain, the *veetha*, the life of those pagan people, something was setting off alarms. I wasn't required on the scene, but I was *curious*. I went down to the holds.

"Cargo officer!" I called out upon arrival, and a man named Nahar popped up in front of me, saluting. "What's going on?"

"Sensors are picking up movement, sir." He started to sweat.

"Movement?" I twisted my face in a grimace. "What have you done so far?"

"Sir. We've pulled everyone out, locked down the cargo bay completely, and confirmed sensors are not malfunctioning. But…"

"But *what?* Spit it out, man."

"Well, sir, the sensors. They're showing movement *everywhere*."

I brushed past him, toward the com stations. "Let me see."

Sure enough, on screen, com was showing red blips moving throughout the hold. All over the grain. *My* grain. My one last hope to avoid being court-martialed. "Damn it. *Enlarge this view.* What the devil are those things?" The com operator zoomed in, but still we saw nothing but small blips on the screen. "Cargo officer, open the hold. I'm going in."

"Sir! Protocol requires —" he stammered, but I cut him off.

"I override protocol. *Do you realize how important this grain is?* Open that goddamned door, or I'll have you thrown in the brig and your replacement will open it."

He did so without another word, and as the hold doors slid with a hiss of air, I stepped in. Nahar followed, quickly closing the doors behind us.

Rushing into the rows of stored grain, I strained my eyes to find what was there. At first, I saw nothing. Then, leaning in close to one pile of *veetha*, I saw them: dozens of miniature versions of the colossus that had destroyed my carriers. And they seemed to be *eating the grain*. "No," I

130

muttered.

Cargo officer Nahar stepped forward, saw what I was seeing and gasped. Then, looking around, we saw them. Hundreds, maybe thousands of them. "That's… impossible," Nahar said. "My men inspected this grain. *I* inspected this grain. Maybe there were flecks of dirt, bits of rock, but not *this*. Nothing even remotely that size would have been overlooked."

I thought a moment. "Then there seems to be only one explanation." He stared at me, eyes wide. "They're growing," I said. I knew what I'd do. It would be a disaster, but we'd purge the hold. Send the little devils to their death in space. I'd figure out a way to salvage my career, even without the damned grain. I started to give the order, when the com officer outside the hold broke in over crackling speakers.

"Sirs! Alarm sensors going off, all over!"

Nahar shouted back, angrily. "We *know*, you imbecile!"

The freighter continued its unstoppable superluminal fall toward Central One, as the com officer breathlessly responded. "Sir, no, sir! Not in the hold, where you are." The speaker crackled again as we looked at each other in confusion. "Sensors are going off *out here*! They're going off all over the ship!"

∞

Time in Time

The creature huddled as deep in the crag of rock as it could, gasping for breath. Its world had turned wrong in many ways, ways it had no ability to comprehend. It didn't know where any of its kind were anymore, or where to find food. The air was heavy, hot, full of dust, making breathing near impossible. The creature didn't think of its impending death, not able to understand the concepts of life or death. It only knew the immediacies of its situation, and its instincts. Its situation was bleak. Its instincts were lost. The creature panted, accidentally sucking in the harsh dust, then it spent several long minutes coughing roughly. It pushed deeper into the rock, wanting to get out of the hot air, though there was no escape. It closed its eyes, and any observer might have thought it dead. But of course, there were no observers. It didn't matter. 5.83 seconds after, the sun of this creature's system went supernova and it was obliterated.

* * *

1.6 billion years later, and 782 trillion kilometers across the universe, the sentient being entered. It had a name, but its name is of no importance. It had a gender, but that, too, is irrelevant. S/He saw the other sentient, and something inherent in its being changed. This was a wholly unexpected change, one that both seemed valuable and oddly intangible to the being, creating a sort of mind-altering confusion. The other also had name, gender. They both had specifics of appearance, personality, and etiquette that aren't germane. Suffice that they existed, and that they met.

At the moment when s/he and s/he first touch, they recall no memory of one another, for they were destroyed. Their organs, the very layers of skin covering their bodies, have no memory of ever touching before, for those organs, too, were destroyed. The cells that make up the organs do not recall a past mutual history, for the cells were ripped apart. The molecules that comprise the cells do not know each other, as they were rent as well. Even the atoms are unaware, given that they were split and broken. All these were unknowing and accurate. But at the subatomic, something was familiar. At this level, there is no such thing as memory, but there may be continuity.

Beyond understanding, a sense bubbles to the surface of the sentient being's consciousness as a feeling of *déjà vu*, of the beings knowing each other sometime before. But they did not, in any normal sense of the words. There was no reason to it, no amount of conversation that could unlock some forgotten past connection. But yet they felt connected.

The subatomic particles within the two beings had a shelf-life, it was certain. However, that shelf-life was long, to the degree that the 1.6 billion years between their meetings was trivial.

There was, even after all the elapsed time, something continuous about their reunion. The beings began a long relationship, though of course the span of their lives was finite as well. When their time expired, their component parts would begin a new journey, perhaps to meet again.

How it was that a collection of twirling and twitching subatomic particles became atoms became molecules became cells became organs became beings and became, sometimes, sentient, was a mystery. But s/he and s/he knew there was something, though they never knew, could never know, that their last meeting was pressed deep against a burning rock, an infinity of time and space ago.

Have a Seat by the Fire

The road, if it could be called that, lay hidden beneath several inches of snow. Making matters worse, the weather had changed overnight, warming up and turning the heavy white mat of snow into a messy slush. As the first rays of sunlight streaked horizontally through the denuded branches along the downhill edge of the road, the sound of her car engine was all that broke the silence on the mountainside. The nearly bald tires of Angela Vengaza's faded green sedan were just north of useless. Still, she made progress, perhaps simply by force of will.

The melting snow was streaked with blotches of brown and orange where another vehicle had left its tracks going up the hill in the early morning. Angela could see the spot where those tracks had abandoned the road and turned left onto a short driveway. Gauging their size and tread, she assumed it was one of the big work trucks common on the farms in these remote hills. She had kept her tires within the tracks for nearly twenty minutes, climbing the hill. It must've been the only thing keeping her from sliding, for, as she passed the point where the tracks left the road, her car drove into the pristine slush and immediately began to fishtail.

Angela did precisely the wrong thing, jabbing her foot at the accelerator and twisting the wheel in a near panic. Even though the slope of the road was relatively slight, the old sedan slid, spinning downhill and colliding sideways into a thick tree with a sound like a heavy sigh. Not so much a crash as a sense of giving up. As Angela collected herself, doing a mental inventory to ensure she wasn't harmed, she considered her situation: she was alone on a remote road in the middle of nowhere, and no one knew she had come here. Still holding the steering wheel, she looked up through the windshield with an expression of intense weariness.

Across the road, a white mailbox read 'JACOBS' in peeling black sticker letters. Behind the mailbox, up the hill, there was a house.

* * *

Raymond Jacobs lived alone, on purpose. He stayed away from people. It wasn't that he disliked most folks, or couldn't hold a decent conversation; he could. But there was something hard about dealing with people that he didn't like. He didn't like the way it made him feel. So he chose to be by himself. It was better that way.

Back when he was younger, when he lived in the city, people called him Ray Jay. It was a name he'd grown to hate. Here in the country, where his nearest neighbor was halfway down the mountain, and probably over two miles away as the crow flies, most people who knew him just called him Jake. He considered telling people to call him Ray, but Ray was his father's name. Jake wasn't much like his father, and something told him he should have a name of his own.

His right knee was bad off, hurt him most days. But days like today were worse. Days when the weather changed. His knee throbbed deep inside, a place that no amount of massaging or rest ever helped. On the bad days, Jake would just sit.

He had made coffee on his tiny electric stove, standing over it favoring his good leg. When the old metal percolator sounded, he snatched it off the hot coil and poured the coffee into his waiting mug. He didn't take sugar or cream. Seemed too snooty for him. Plus, the coffee he could afford was *bad*. Stuff the supermarket in town probably couldn't sell to customers, so they offloaded it to the little general stores that pocked the surrounding hills. Jake drank the swill black because at least then it had some kind of *flavor*. Bad, in Jake's mind, was at least a flavor. He preferred bad to bland. It was one of his major failings.

Using his cane, he limped to the wood stove, opened the door, and stoked the fire. The wood stove was the only heat in his small mountain home. Keeping it burning was something he did offhand, like breathing. After he was content with the state of the fire, he closed the door and returned to the kitchen.

On the same, still-hot burner where he had made coffee, he cooked himself a couple of eggs and reheated two sausage links. Finally, he sat at his little metal table, eating and looking out the window. When a dribble of egg yolk fell on the flowered, plastic tablecloth, he absently dabbed at it with the square of paper towel he was using as a napkin.

Jake sipped the awful coffee, hissing air between his teeth to cool it as he drank, and noticed the sound.

The hum of an engine, coming up the mountain.

At first, he assumed it was Terry, the guy who lived over the next rise. Sometimes Terry would hit the general store in the valley during the early morning, then head back to his farm with some food and a copy of the local newspaper. The paper gave Terry something to bitch about, reading stories about how the county government was wasting tax dollars on one thing or another.

But this engine sounded different. Unfamiliar.

Jake straightened his back to stare down the yard toward the road. He saw his own tire tracks, where he'd gone out to replenish his supply of the third-rate coffee earlier that morning. Only his tracks. Meaning that Terry had not come over the mountain.

Leaning forward, he watched the road. Jake lived far enough away from other people that a strange car was something of note. Finally, it came into view, sliding and wagging through the slushy snow. A dilapidated light green economy car, probably 20 years old at least, was creeping up the snow-covered road. Jake sighed, thinking the car had no business on his mountain, certainly not in the snow. He figured it was only a matter of time before someone would be pulling the car and its hapless driver out of a ditch. If the driver was lucky enough to live through the crash.

No sooner had he had this thought than Jake saw the car pass his driveway. And in the unblemished snow, it started to go out of control. "Ah, shit," he muttered to himself.

Jake watched with mixed emotions, part smug satisfaction at being right, part annoyance at the intrusion, as the car fell off the road and looped around, swinging into one of the trees near the base of his driveway with a *paaah*. Sitting at his little kitchen table, Jake's expression remained the same. He didn't stand.

He waited a moment.

Get out of the car. You're okay. And then, get the damned thing started and drive away.

He waited another moment. And the driver's door opened.

A young woman, pretty, dark hair flowing over the collar of her white parka, got out. She kicked the door closed with a loud *thud*. From his vantage, he saw her mouth moving but couldn't hear what she was saying. He assumed it wasn't words meant for general consumption.

The woman stood, hands on her hips, looking at the car.

Then her head turned, and she looked in his direction. Reflexively, he slouched back down in his chair, trying not to be seen. Still, his eyes peered over the sill, and he saw the woman, the very attractive brunette, start walking toward him.

"Shit," he said again.

* * *

Angela trudged through the sloppy melting snow, toward the front door. In the driveway, she passed the truck, the one whose tracks she had been driving in, parked close to the house. It was a massive, dark blue thing, jacked up off the ground so far that Angela doubted she could even get in it without a ladder. She stepped past the truck and toward the house, seeing the faded red paint peeling off the door's cheap aluminum surface.

She looked for a doorknob or bell, but there was none. Instead, she opened the rickety screen door and knocked. For a moment, there was no answer.

Angela stepped back, hesitant and somewhat unsure of herself. The truck's tracks were fresh, surely from only a couple of hours before. Someone had to be home.

Finally, she heard the sound of a lock being undone, then another. *Clack, shhhh, clack.* Then the knob turned and the door slowly opened.

A grey-haired man peered at her, hunched over on a cane. He limped awkwardly backward to allow the door to open. He wasn't ancient, but he was old. A big man, who earlier in his life was most likely large and imposing. Now his size seemed to be a detriment, as if it weighed him down on his creaking bones. His skin was pale and wrinkled, pocked with dark spots and loose in places. His mostly bald head held wisps of white hair. Suddenly, she realized she had been staring, so she awkwardly blinked her eyes and spoke.

"Uh, hi... can I use your phone? I sort of wrecked my car," she said, pointing over her shoulder and down the drive to where the car could easily be seen resting against the tree. The old man blinked, saying nothing.

Angela waited a moment, locking eyes with him. Seeing his eyes that were not lost or senile. Eyes that held her stare with an energy she couldn't describe. "Hello?" She made a little wave, trying to get some reaction.

"Come in," he said, far too gruffly, stepping forward a bit to push open the screen, then slouching back into his tiny living room. Angela grabbed the handle and stepped up and into the small house.

For a moment, she froze, looking around the room, not even breathing. Then, with a loud *bang*, the door slammed behind her making her jump, startled by the sound and letting out a gasp.

The man turned and looked at her, and she sheepishly looked back. "Sorry," she said with a nervous giggle, as she thumbed a gesture at the door behind her.

The man turned away. "Cold," he said harshly.

Angela tilted her head. "I'm sorry?" The man turned back slightly.

"Cold today," he said. "Warmer than yesterday, but still damn cold." He looked at her, waiting.

She nodded a little, nervously. "Yeah," Angela said, shivering unconsciously.

"Well," he said, walking toward the kitchen, "have a seat by the fire." Offhandedly, he gestured toward the wood stove. Angela realized she actually was cold. The heater in her beat-up car was mostly shot, and she had been standing out in the snow. She sidled up to the gas stove and sat in a folding chair that had been left there. *Have a seat by the fire.* She mused at the pleasantry. *So nice of you to offer, thank you. Creep.*

A *single* folding chair. This man was clearly not used to having company. Angela looked around the small room: the stove, the chair, a small television on a cheap particleboard stand, and a few magazines in a stack. To the side, a basic square kitchen table acted as a border between the living room and the kitchen space. Warming herself by the fire, Angela watched the man limp into the kitchen.

"Coffee?" he asked. Angela's head snapped up, with a guilty look as if she'd been caught going through his possessions.

"Um, yes, sure, thank you," she stammered. She watched the old man open a cabinet and rattle through it. Finally he came away with a faded old mug and plunked it down on the Formica countertop. He dropped a percolator onto the electric burner and turning the heat on with a click.

The old man hobbled to the kitchen table, taking the single chair and moving it to the side opposite Angela. He sat and looked at her through his bushy eyebrows. "You need to make a call?"

Shaking her head, she sat upright suddenly. "Oh. Yes! Do you have a phone I could use? I'd really appreciate it." She offered her most polite smile. The man simply rolled his eyes toward his left. There on the wall, with a long, spiraling cord hanging down, was a lime green plastic telephone. Angela walked over hurriedly and picked it up. She unbuttoned her white parka but left it on, warmer now from the heat of the stove.

She dialed a series of numbers, then idly waited for some response. Once or twice, she pulled the phone away from her ear and pushed more buttons on its cheap curved interior, until finally something connected. On the stove, the coffee pot started bubbling, and the old man pushed back from the table to attend to it. Angela turned toward the window and put a finger in one ear to block the noise. She spoke into the phone, asking for help and offering details about her location. Finally, she uttered profuse thanks and hung up the phone. She turned back to the table and saw the old man sitting again, a mug of coffee in one hand, the other mug steaming and waiting for her across the table. She noticed that he was staring at her. It was distinctly uncomfortable.

There was no second chair at the table, and at first Angela looked confused. Then the old man nodded his head toward the chair by the fire. *Of course*, Angela thought. She lifted the flimsy folding chair, moved it beside the table, then sat in front of her coffee.

"I'm warning you," he said in an ominous tone that made her stop a moment. "It's bad. But it's the best I can afford."

Not wanting to offend, she simply smiled. "Thank you so much for your hospitality," she said, idly stirring the coffee with a spoon the man had sat next to her mug, though there was no sugar or milk to stir in. "They said they can be here in an hour. Will that be okay?" She looked up.

The old man nodded once. "Name's Jake. You?"

She froze for a second, losing all hints of her smile while looking at the old man. After a moment, he noticed her hesitation and stared at her again through his bushy brows. "Renee," she replied. "Renee Stevens. Thank you again for your help." Her polite smile returned, though strained.

* * *

Liar, he thought. *You're no more of a Renee than I am.* Still Jake nodded and accepted the false name. "Nice to meet you, Renee." He went back to studying his coffee. *She's afraid of me*, he thought. *Probably smart of her.*

"Jake," she said. "Is that for *Jacobs*?" she asked.

Jake raised one eyebrow. *How the hell does she know my name?* He paused, scratching his chin and staring at her. *But damn, she does look familiar.* "Do I know you?" he asked, brows raised.

"Oh no, sorry," she said, gingerly sipping the coffee and wincing a bit at the taste. "It's on your mailbox."

Jake huffed, annoyed at himself for forgetting something so simple. "Yeah, Jake for Jacobs. My first name's Raymond, but nobody calls me that."

The girl nodded in a strangely rough way.

Jake was old and hobbled, but he still outweighed the young woman, "*Renee*," by well over a hundred pounds, and even hunched, he must've been eight inches taller. With his large frame slouched over the little table, he looked like a vulture hovering over its next meal. Up close, he realized the woman was probably in her thirties, with a sort of natural beauty he imagined would last her for several more decades. *If she lives so long*, Jake thought.

The awkward pair sat in silence, randomly sipping coffee. So near, they pretended not to notice anything while simultaneously studying each other closely. As he lifted his mug, Jake allowed himself a long look at her face.

Tina. Damn, she looks like Tina. Oh God. That's who she reminds me of: Tina. Tina and Ray Jay.

Jake shuddered involuntarily, then, noticing her looking at him, he faked a couple of coughs. "Coffee went down the wrong pipe," he lied.

"Are you okay?" she asked

Jake didn't reply buy simply waved his hand.

After a moment, he abruptly spoke. "Where'ya from?"

"The city," she replied, offering nothing more. Jake wasn't surprised. She looked city. He remembered how they looked there, how they dressed. How they talked.

"What brings you up the mountain, *Renee*?" He almost called her Tina.

She paused a moment before responding. "I think I got lost. I was trying to get to my cousin's place over in Kingston."

Jake laughed a gruff little laugh. "Kingston?" He huffed. "Yeah, you're lost." He took the last sip of his coffee.

The woman looked at him with her striking brown eyes. "How do you come to live here?" she asked.

Well, that's a strange question, he thought.

* * *

Angela held the old man's stare. But suddenly, it hit her: she was very much afraid. She was in the home of a complete stranger, in the middle of nowhere, and this man, though old, was much bigger than her. She thought he probably saw through her fake name very easily. As a single bead of sweat appeared on her upper lip, she wondered if she should simply go. She wiped the sweat away before the old man could see it. The stove was warm, but not that warm.

143

No, she thought. *I'm not going to walk out like a scared little chickenshit girl.*

She waited for him to answer. He looked annoyed. "You know how some days, nothing goes your way?" he asked. Angela nodded slightly. "Well, that's true for some *lives*, too."

Angela's grip on the mug tightened, her knuckles turning white.

Jake continued. "I was never very smart, never well educated. But I did all right." He nodded to emphasize the point. "I used to live in the city. Held a bunch of different jobs, God, I can't even remember them all. But if you were to ask me what I did, I'd have to say I was a builder. Give me the plans and I could build almost anything." He paused. "Well, not *machines*, but buildings, houses, you know, that stuff. I could build anything. I did a ton of different things on job sites: masonry, carpentry, whatever they needed. And so, I could usually find work pretty easy." *Which meant that if you got fired for fighting or mouthing off, you could always find something new*, she thought, eyeing his formidable size. Angela nodded her head slightly, telling him to continue. Her jaw was set tight.

With an effort, he got up, taking the mug to the sink. "Anyways, in those days, I'd usually have a pocket full of money on Friday evening, and a strong desire to see if I could use it up by Monday. I wasn't much for planning ahead." He plunked his mug down in the sink, then turned back to her. "More coffee?" he asked with eyebrows raised.

Angela shook her head. "No, thanks," she said through clenched teeth, trying to force a smile. Her cup was still nearly full, the brown liquid bitter and awful tasting.

"Anyways, one Friday, I met this girl, Tina." He paused, almost wistfully. Angela's lip quivered just slightly. *One hour*, she thought. *I've got one hour. Even less now.*

"Tina didn't belong in that place, sitting on a barstool patched with duct tape. She seemed better, classier." He limped back to the table and sat down with a *whoomp*. "I have no idea how I caught her eye. But I did."

Angela's mug suddenly crashed to the floor, breaking into pieces and spilling the remains of her coffee. "I am *so sorry!*" She jumped up, trying to hide how flustered she was. "Do you have a dustpan? Paper towels?" Jake started to rise. "No, please, sit. I'll clean it up. Just tell me where to find things." He pointed.

Angela grabbed the paper towels first and mopped the soaked floor. After she threw the wet paper towels in the little metal cylindrical trash can, she grabbed the dustpan and brush from where Jake pointed, under the sink. On her hands and knees under the small kitchen table, she swept the broken shards into the pan. Just as she was about to stand, she looked at Jake's legs, in the shadow under the table.

There, strapped to one calf, was a small gun.

* * *

Jake sat at the table, watching the young woman clean up her mess. As she swept under the table, he saw her body tense for a moment. He wasn't surprised. He knew what she saw. Jake was a person used to intimidating others. He didn't even spare an emotion for it; it simply was *expected.*

The woman finished cleaning up, dumped the fragments of the mug into the trashcan, and resumed her seat across from him at the kitchen table. He looked at the cheap old clock on the wall. A half hour had passed. She'd be gone soon. Pity.

She looked *so much* like Tina. Jake had to stop himself from staring. Just like the first time he met Tina in the bar, this woman, this '*Renee,*' seemed out of place. In the hovel he called home, she seemed almost regal. In some way, he was back. Back in love with Tina. In another way, it made him want to kill this *Renee.* Like he had killed Tina.

Why did I do it? he mused to himself. It was a question he sometimes asked in self-pity. But he knew the answer. *Because you were jealous. And stupid.* The heat of the moment, the drugs, but in the end, the final straw was *him.* It always came down to him: what would he do? Even he didn't know, most of the time.

145

Tina and Ray Jay, dammit, we were good. Why did we fall apart? Jake thought. *She had to go and tell me.* Jake muttered a curse under his breath.

The woman stopped and locked eyes with him, until Jake quickly looked away.

* * *

Angela stole a look at her watch as she sat. *Less than a half hour*, she told herself. *I can do this.*

"Tell me more about her... did you say her name was Tina?" Angela asked. The old man nodded. "What'd she look like?" Angela looked away quickly.

The old man stared at her. "You know, she looked a bit like you. Which is probably why I brought her up. I haven't spoken her name in, hell, *years*, I guess."

Angela looked away, studying the leg of the table beside her, focusing on its clouded metal texture. *Why am I even talking? I don't want to hear what he has to say*, she thought.

Reflexively, with a tiny moment of panic, she reached into her pocket. Then, just as quickly, she pulled her hand out and brushed a few hairs back from her face.

No, that's wrong. I do want to hear what he has to say. "Where is she now?" Angela asked, cringing a bit.

Jake turned away. "Dead," he said, gruffly. He started to stand, but stumbled and fell toward the table. At the last moment, he caught himself with one large hand, slamming into the center of the table. Angela jumped. Getting the cane under him to help support his weight, Jake staggered away from the table, toward the kitchen counter behind him. He opened another cupboard and pulled out two small glasses, then grabbed for a bottle of brown liquid on the counter. Turning back to the table, he worked the cane with one hand while holding the bottle in the other. The two glasses dangled from his fingers, jangling on the bottle as he limped.

Angela saw the bottle was some kind of scotch. *Well*, she thought, *seems a tad early in the day.*

Jake thumped the bottle on the table, followed by the two glasses. As he dropped into the chair, he said, "If we're going to talk about these things, I'm gonna need a drink."

* * *

The woman — he didn't even want to think of her as Renee, since he was certain that wasn't her name — said nothing as he poured the cheap scotch. Jake downed the shot without even putting the bottle down, then poured himself a second. Cradling his second shot, he saw the woman pick up her first and sip at it. She winced a bit at the burn.

For Jake, the burn was inside. A spreading warmth, a feeling of new energy. It reminded him of his younger days. Spinning the glass idly, he spoke. "Me and Tina were together for two years. She was good for me, then, at least in the beginning. She kept me calm. Before I met her, I'd get in some kind of fight just about every weekend. Some week days, too. But with her…" He took a little sip, egging himself on. "With her, I was able to let things go. I wouldn't fight because things bothered me less." Jake looked out the window, seeing the sun break through clouds and bounce bright beams off the white snow. *That road's gonna get worse*, he thought. *This woman may be stuck here longer than she thinks.*

"How did she die?" The voice of the woman snapped him out his momentary daze. He turned to look back at her, and was surprised to see her glass empty. Without asking, he poured her a second, emptied his own glass, and poured himself a third.

"She left me. At first, I didn't know why. I took it pretty bad." Jake rubbed the bridge of his nose, closing his eyes momentarily to bring back the memories. He chuckled a little. "There were guys, that first weekend when she left, I must've beat nearly to death, and they probably didn't do a thing to me. Just took it out on them." He downed the third shot, and when he spoke again, his voice was stronger. "She was gone for months. I didn't even hear rumors about where she went. It was sort of like when I first met her, she was dropped from the sky. She was just *there* one day. And like that, one day she was just *gone*."

'Renee' tilted back her head and drained the second shot. "How'd she die?" she repeated.

Jake tilted his head and made a wry smirk. "Like I said, for months she was just gone. Then one day, a friend told me he had seen her across town. But he was nervous. He didn't want to tell me something. But I had a *persuasive* way about me. Finally, he said. He had seen her, and she was *pregnant*. I forced him to tell me every detail of where and when he saw her, then I got there in a hurry." *I always did prefer to be bad.*

Suddenly, the energy left him. He reached for the bottle and unscrewed the cap. With jittering hands, he poured again, giving her another once again without asking.

"I found her. And…" He took the shot, then squeezed the empty glass in his huge hand so hard that the thing seemed like it might shatter. Jake looked the young woman in the eyes. "And I laid my hands upon her." He sat, stone faced, saying nothing more.

"You killed her," the woman said softly. It wasn't a question.

"No," Jake said. *Yes*, he thought. He cleared his throat. "No, I laid my hands on her. She was screaming. Someone called the cops. And for that I left town and never came back. But I didn't kill her." *Yes, I did*, he thought.

* * *

Yes, you did, Angela thought. She considered the shot of scotch in front of her, once, then again, then decided against it. She needed her wits about her. She was dealing with a killer.

A long moment of silence fell like a fog, filling the room. Angela sat perfectly still, while inside her every nerve was on fire, tensed and alert.

She feigned looking calmly around the room. Still she had to ask. "What about the baby?"

The old man shook his head. "I didn't hurt any damn baby."

"Whose baby was it?" she asked, holding back the flood of her emotions. She could barely keep her hand from shaking where she held the glass, so she put her hands in her lap hoping he wouldn't notice.

"No idea. Probably a good thing, though. If I knew who the guy was, I *definitely* woulda killed him."

Angela tensed. *Say it*, she thought. *Say it*.

"What if it was *yours*?" she asked, her voice coming out as a growl. The old man, the old fool, looked up, stunned. *He's really never thought of that before. Son of a bitch.*

Jake looked rattled, but after a moment, he shook it off. "No way," he said. Still he poured another shot, hands trembling again. "No way," he muttered, lower.

"When did it happen?" Angela asked, eyes locked on the old man.

He leaned back in his chair, causing it to creak in protest. "God, many years. Thirty, maybe? Thirty years ago. You probably weren't even born." Jake chuckled again, peering at the young woman through his white brows. Suddenly, he froze. Angela was staring at him with a raw hatred that even he couldn't fail to see it.

"You're right," she spat out. "I *wasn't* even born."

Reaching into the pocket of her parka, Angela pulled out a gun and trained it on the middle of Jake's chest.

"What the f—!"

"*Shut your mouth*," she said, cutting him off. "I've heard enough of what you have to say. And you know who I am."

* * *

Tina had a daughter, he thought. *But how? I know I killed her.*

"Don't hurt your little brain trying to figure it out. When they took her to the hospital, they saved me. *They delivered me from the womb of my dead mother.*" The gun shook as she spoke, so full of anger.

"What's your real name?" Jake asked. "I know it's not *Renee*." The booze had the effect of both steadying him and making him care less about the bullet that might end his life.

"Angela Vengaza, not that that'll matter to you."

"Don't know that name," Jake said.

"How would you? I don't even know where the name came from. It was on some paperwork, and just stuck. So yeah, *Renee* was a lie. But so is Angela. I don't *have a name*, thanks to *you*." Then she raised the gun and steadied it, the dark hollow of its barrel looking like the pit of eternity facing him.

She's gonna shoot me, he thought. *But not if I can help it.* Jake sat still for just a moment more.

And then, quicker than he had moved in many years, he jumped.

* * *

Angela expected him to try, but she wasn't sure how. Suddenly, Jake knocked over the bottle of scotch, splashing the liquid at her. Some stung her eyes and she blinked, reeling backward. With his other hand, Jake reached toward his ankle.

His gun, she reminded herself.

She fired.

In the small room, her gun made a deafening pop. Jake both lurched and fell backward onto the kitchen floor, taking the table down with him in a huge crash and breaking of glass. Angela staggered up and away, toward the wood stove. Jake's large frame slid and left a streak of red across the floor.

In a moment, all was still. The acrid smell of gunpowder mixed with the strong odor of the scotch. Angela waited, still holding the gun out in front of her. Jake was making low, gurgling moans on the kitchen floor, sounds of the dying. His body was curled behind the overturned table.

Angela stepped forward, wanting to see his face, the look on his stupid face. The beast, slain by the beauty with no real name. Killed by his own daughter. She hated to think of herself as his daughter, but it was the only true identity she really had. Looking over the edge of the table, she caught his eye.

Jake seemed unable to turn. He was lying on his right side, one arm pinned below him. He was forced to look at her sideways. She saw a trickle of blood come from his open mouth, matching the color of the pool forming at his back. *Die, you bastard. And die in pain, the way you killed my mother.* Angela allowed herself a vicious smile.

And Jake raised his right hand. It wasn't pinned after all. It held the small gun she had seen strapped to his ankle. Before she could react, he fired.

Oh God Oh God Oh God, was all she could think as pain tore into her shoulder, ripping through the parka and splattering her own blood, red on the white coat. She fell backward, knocking over the pathetic stack of magazines that sat near the wood stove. For a moment, she writhed, clutching at the terrible pain there. Then she heard a shuffling sound, and she knew Jake was trying to stand. Angela bit down on her lip, hard, drawing fresh blood. Pain now shot from two places on her body, but the effect steadied her just enough. She rolled and flopped up on her knees.

Jake struggled in the kitchen, trying to get the cane under him. He slipped and fell again. She saw clearly what he had become: a monster laid low not so much by her bullet as by time. He reminded her of a turtle turned over, desperately trying to flip off of its own shell, damned by its own body.

She stood and strode back to him, ignoring the pain, ignoring the blood pouring down her arm and onto the cheap linoleum floor. Jake struggled again, trying to rise, but she was there.

Standing above him, she raised her gun again. "This is for her. For Tina. The mother I never knew." Angela put the gun barrel just inches from Jake's thick skull.

"Go to hell," Jake muttered, spitting blood.

"You first," she said with a sneer. "Oh, and when you get there, have a seat by the fire."

Walking on the Spot

The young man descended the flight of stairs quickly, burst through the door, and launched himself out into the summer day. Around him, the city hummed. He scanned the street and jogged across. Midway, he felt a chill, not on his skin, but inside, like when he swallowed a big mouthful of ice cream. He shivered but ran on, to the other side of the road where the stairs led to the subway.

He had probably run across the street hundreds of times, always a little differently because of other pedestrians, cars, bikes, and the general crowded nature of the city. But on occasion, he felt the chill. It was always about a step before the manhole cover. The one that read CMT PWR CO. The cold air must have blown up from underneath the ground somehow.

Down the stairs he went, not running, but moving fast, because he could. He pulled out his card, passed the turnstile and went to the platform. The northbound train was just arriving, and he stepped aboard. He had no newspaper or book. No phone or reader or game device. He watched the people. He watched out the windows, at the streaks of light passing. He thought of everything and nothing, at once. The train arrived at his

153

destination and he stepped off.

At street level, he took a left, made his way to a familiar door, and rang the bell.

After a moment, the old man opened the door.

"Grandson, thank you for coming," the old man said.

"Certainly," the young man replied. "Is everything okay?"

The old man sighed, waiving the younger inside. "Things are as they are." The young man didn't understand the meaning of this, but he was used to the old man sometimes saying things beyond his comprehension.

As the young man walked in, his back naturally stiffened. For inside his grandfather's home, they adhered to a more rigid formality. It was not impersonal, not disconnected, simply more formal.

They walked into the small kitchen and sat at the small, square table.

"May I make you some tea?"

The young man nodded. "Thank you, grandfather." As the old man shuffled around the kitchen, preparing the tea, the young man sat quietly. He watched the old man, looked at the details of the old kitchen. He was a young man but he knew things were impermanent. He often liked to stare and memorize things, so that, if they one day disappeared, he would still have them in his mind.

The pot whistled and the old man poured the steaming water into two cups. He brought the cups to the table and sat down across from the young man. They blew on the hot liquid, then sipped around the flecks of tea leaves floating in their cups, making polite slurping noises for a few minutes.

Finally, the old man spoke. "Do you believe in reading tea leaves?"

"No. Truthfully, I do not." The young man blew again, then sipped.

"Nor I. Seems awfully random if you ask me."

"Agreed. Also, what happens if I have two cups of tea? The leaves do not match. Which one is right? Which is wrong?"

"There is no validation. You cannot verify the prediction."

"Yes. Though I suppose those who believe in reading tea leaves would say you must have faith."

"Bah. I like things to make more sense than that."

"Me too."

"Which I why I think we've always gotten along well."

"Well, it is one reason."

"Yes."

They sat in silence again, still blowing on the tea, sipping. Finally, as they each finished, one after the other, they each took their cup to the sink, rinsed it and wiped it, then set it upside down to dry on the rack.

"Grandfather?"

"Yes?"

"Was there something special you wanted to do today?"

"Oh definitely."

"What?"

"I'm afraid I cannot say, or at least not come right out and say."

The young man was used to his grandfather's ways. "Okay. When you are ready. Is there something I should do to prepare?"

"That is a hard question to answer. The short response is 'no,' however, we have known each other a long time. Your entire life, in fact. So the more correct answer may be 'yes,' though only you can answer."

"I do not understand."

"You will."

"When?"

"I will start to explain." The old man walked out of the kitchen, into the living room, and sat in a comfortable but small chair beside a low table. The young man joined him, sitting in a matching chair across. It dawned on the young man that they always sat this way, across from each other, like a mirror was placed between them where they sat, each reflecting the other, but at a different moment in time. He looked at the old man and saw his future reflection. He studied the lined hands and the wrinkles around his face. The wisps of white hair that no longer formed a complete cover for his head, revealing small spots here and there. He noticed that the old man's ear lobes were a little long, at least longer than he could recall noticing before.

But more than anything, the young man noticed the old man was ready for something. His hair, though thin, was neatly combed. His fingernails each trimmed and possibly even filed smooth. He wore familiar clothes, for the old man had only so many articles of clothing. But the ones he had chosen for this day were probably his nicest, at least nicest in terms of things to wear on a regular day. He did not don a jacket, but his button-up shirt was neatly ironed. His pants were pressed, and his shoes shone. This was remarkable, for every man has his faults. The young man had never known the old man to care particularly about the state of his shoes. To see these shoes, old and a little worn, but shined and glossy, was a surprise.

Still he knew his grandfather, and therefore knew his grandfather had reasons for what he did. They would be revealed in time. The young man sat up straight, echoing the straight back of the old man, awaiting what he had to say.

"You do not believe in reading tea leaves."

"Correct, as we just discussed."

"Yes, but there are other means of seeing what the future may hold."

"Perhaps there are, though I cannot think of any that are completely reliable."

"I can think of one."

"What is it?"

"I think I need to back up before I tell you. If I just tell you, you may not believe me."

"Do you think I distrust you? I do not."

"No, I do not think that. I just wish for you to have more information, so that you may better understand what I have to say."

"All right. I am listening."

"Good. Did you ever meet my mother? I think you did."

"I think I did, also, but I was very young. I do not mean any insult, but I do not remember."

"There is no insult. My mother was a very fine woman, very smart, very capable. She also took it upon herself to ensure that the family kept certain traditions. Actually, these are more than traditions, for traditions may just be simple rituals that a family performs year after year, generation after generation. My mother did more than simply maintain rituals."

"I see."

"No, not yet, you do not. My mother also made sure that we understood certain mysteries of the world, which could not be described or rationalized in a normal way, for any normal explanation of them did not make sense. Still, over generations of observation, these mysteries maintained recognizable patterns, which people like my mother, and her mother before her, and, so I am told, her grandfather before that, documented. Or at least remembered."

The young man remained silent. He could tell that pleasantries such as 'I understand' would only result in his grandfather realizing and therefore pointing out that he actually did not understand. Which he did not. Still, after a moment, he realized the old man was not continuing, and so he felt obligated to say something. "What were these things they remembered?"

"Oh, many things. My mother's grandfather would be your great-great-great-grandfather. So you can see this has been happening for quite a long while."

The young man just nodded.

"They remembered things about the world from a long time ago, that most others have forgotten. Things most others might even notice or experience, but then ignore. I do not know if these things are remembered outside of our family, for I have never had this discussion before. Only when my mother told me did I learn these things, and only now when I am talking with you will I pass it along."

"What about my father? Did you tell him about these things?"

"No. I am sorry that I did not. He may have found out for himself, but I did not tell him in time before he died."

"Found out for himself? How so?"

"Hold on a moment. So, this is the part I have to tell you that you may not believe. At least not yet. Have you ever had a dream that you were dying?"

"Yes, I think. I do not tend to remember my dreams, but I think I have dreamed that before, yes. Why?"

"Because it is possible to dream of the exact way you will die."

"But, grandfather, I've dreamed of flying, and outer space, and becoming a werewolf. None of those things are true."

"Absolutely correct. It is not those kinds of dreams that contain truth. Let me ask you: can you *think* of something that is untrue?"

"Certainly. I can think of many things that are untrue, nearly unlimited things that are untrue."

"Ah, but can you also think of things that are true?"

"Yes, of course."

"So, why should dreams be any different? They are stories in your mind. Some of the are farcical and impossible, but some are completely and utterly true."

"I am sorry, grandfather. I find that difficult to believe. Just a short while ago, in the kitchen, you asked me about tea leaves. And you yourself said 'There is no validation. You cannot verify the prediction.' Have you changed your mind?"

"No, not at all. Because there is a way to verify the prediction."

"There is a way to verify a dream in which you die? How?"

"Well, the most obvious answer is that you die."

"Okay, but even still. If you were to have a dream of dying, then to die in that certain way, how would this be verifiable? First, it could still be a coincidence. And second, you would be dead, so there would be no one to do the verification."

"All true. But…" The old man paused and the young man waited. "But what if you were not the only one to know the dream."

"Are you suggesting some kind of shared dream?"

"No, no, no, not at all. That sounds like magic, and I am not talking about magic. I'm talking about time. Do you think time only goes in one direction?"

"I have never considered the question."

"Okay, consider it now."

"I do not know. I only am aware of time moving in one direction, it is the only definition of time I can verify, so I suppose that I will have to say it is the only way time can behave."

"Do you believe our solar system spins in an arm of the Milky Way galaxy?"

"Yes."

"Why?"

"There is science about it. It has been proven."

"Yes, but you cannot observe it yourself. In fact, no one so far born can observe this."

"But we can see the density of stars, understand the logic of it."

"True, but that's somewhat different from observing it, is it not?"

"Yes, it is."

"Well, I realize I am asking you to consider a number of strange things, but try to believe for a moment that time does not only travel in one direction. For example, you and I look quite a bit alike."

"I have thought that before, too."

"And I have told you how you remind me of me as a young man."

"Yes."

"In a way, that seems like a window backward in time."

"Sure, but that is only a reflection and memory. Time, for us both, continues to move forward."

"True. True. But what if dreams — sometimes — provided a way to skim along time, sometimes backward, sometimes forward, like rewinding or fast-forwarding through a movie? Yes, there is a lot of noise, as if the channel keeps changing while you are zipping back and forth, and that makes it harder to understand what is real and what is not.

But sometimes there are markers."

"Again, I do not understand."

The old man just nodded, now looking much more serious. "There is an old phrase, 'walking on the spot.' Have you heard this?"

"Perhaps once or twice. I think some of the older generation have used it. It seems to be an omen of some kind, to them."

"Yes. Most people use it incorrectly. But we don't. 'Walking on the spot' means that you have found the place where you will die."

The young man leaned back in his chair. He had never heard his grandfather talk about such things. He began to wonder. To consider if the words the old man was saying were not really his own. Though he felt a deep sense of guilt for the idea, he began to question his grandfather's hold on sanity. The pressed and polished appearance. The mystical topic of conversation. Had something inside the old man's brain finally snapped?

"I can tell what you are thinking, grandson."

"Oh?"

"You are wondering if I have finally lost my mind. Or, more precisely, if my mind has finally caught up to my body in age. I can assure you that is not the case. As I said, there are some things where a normal explanation does not make sense."

"So your mother told you about 'walking on the spot,' and now you are telling me?"

"Yes, well mostly that is correct. My mother told me. Her mother told her, and before that, her grandfather told her mother. I cannot say how each of them reacted. But I can tell you how I did. I was like you. I completely and utterly did not believe it."

"Is it that obvious?"

"Yes, grandson, I know you well by now. And like me before you, echoing another moment in time, you are skeptical with good reason. But, just like me, you may find reasons very soon."

"How?"

"I want us to go on a short journey together."

"Where?"

"Not far. There is a park, the Franklin Street Park, a short distance north of here. We can take the bus. I think we can be there in forty minutes or so."

"Why do you want to go there?"

"You know that I used to live in that area, yes?"

"That sounds familiar, though I can only really recall you living here."

"Ah, yes, it was from a time before you were born. But it is true. For more than ten years, I lived near this park."

"I still do not understand why you want to go there and I do not understand what it has to do with everything you have been talking about today."

"You will, grandson."

The old man led the young man. They gathered a few things, nothing more than necessary to take a short ride. Some money, the keys to the house. They left the house and went to the bus stop on the larger street just to the east, where they wordlessly waited a few moments for the bus to arrive.

As the engine roared then slightly diminished, the brakes squealed a high-pitched note, the doors hissed open, and they stepped aboard. It was busy and there was no place to sit. The many faces around them remained self-absorbed, looking at newspapers and phone screens. No one even stood to allow the old man a seat. They stood together near the door, holding a bar above their heads.

"Is there something at this park you wish to show?"

"It is something like that."

"A statue? A marker? Something historic? Something from when you lived in the area?"

"No, nothing like that."

"Then what?"

"My spot."

"Your what? Oh, you mean, spot, like 'walking on the spot?' Like the things you were telling me?"

"Yes." The old man's head hung low for a minute, then, deliberately he raised it. His back stiffened and he stood straighter and more dignified. "Yes. My spot is there."

"The place where you think you are going to die some day?"

"Yes."

"Then why go there?"

"You will see."

They passed the remainder of the trip in silence. The young man faced out the window as the buildings, streets, pedestrians, cars went by, but he did not see them. His grandfather's actions were troublesome. The young man enjoyed his visits because they were structured, and therefore the absolute opposite of stress. Everything was as expected, as it should be. But not this visit. This visit was very, very different. Strange words, and even stranger, this bus, this trip to a park for reasons he scoffed at as ridiculous. 'The spot?' he mused to himself, and nearly he made an expression of disdain. Only his lifelong respect for his grandfather kept it from his face.

The bus stopped.

"I am here," the old man said, but it did not seem that he said it to the young man. They got off the bus.

Frustrated but unsure how to stop this farcical activity, the young man followed his grandfather off the bus, into the park, to a bench. The old man sat, his back rigid and proper. The young man sat beside him, and again from respect, allowed time to pass.

"I know you do not believe what I have said to you."

"I am sorry, grandfather. Validation. Verification. I do not see either. My eyes tell me this is nothing but a place. We are nowhere but a park."

"This is not the spot."

"Then why are we here?" The young man threw his hands up, unable to contain his emotion.

The old man winced, but a restrained wince, one of guilt for putting his grandson through this ordeal. "Grandson, it is time." He pointed. "Do you see the pathway, there by the light post?"

The young man looked. He saw a pathway. He saw several light posts. He looked for something remarkable but saw nothing.

"The post I mean is the one with the green sign."

The young man saw the one. "What does it signify? The pathway? The post? Does the sign say something I should read?"

"No. None of them are important. But in the pathway next to that post is my spot."

"Grandfather, you must realize how this sounds."

"I do. But I have not told you how I know my spot. It is cold. A cold that is always there, day or night, winter and summer. Others will not feel it, if you should ask, but you always will."

"There are cold spots in many places."

"But only this one have I dreamed about. With you, sitting on this bench, on this day."

"This is why you have brought me here today?"

"It is."

"Grandfather, I have never known you to make such outrageous statements. I do not know what to say of it."

"I know. I did not either, when my mother showed me her spot. And told me about her dream. But I understood when she died."

"Are you saying that you will walk on that spot, today, and you will die?"

"Yes."

"Grandfather, please. We need to go home. You are not well."

"Perhaps I am not. I do not know. I presume there must be some reason that will be given for my death, but I do not know it. I feel fine."

"You are serious?"

"I am."

The young man waited, unsure. The old man nearly stood, but something stopped him.

"Then we must go home, right away. If you think you are in danger here, that you could die upon this spot, on this very day, then we must go!"

"This is not the way of things, grandson. I do not understand that part myself, but it is not possible for me to go home now."

"Please, please stop, grandfather. We must go."

"I cannot."

Another pause.

"Then go! Walk on this damned spot, and prove to yourself that this magic is a lie! Do it, if you will not listen to reason!"

"Grandson, release your anger, but I hope that we can find peace between us before I go."

The young man had no words, no idea what to do. Never had he known a situation so ridiculous, yet so grave. "I am sorry, grandfather. I do not mean to yell at you."

"You do mean to yell at me, and it is understandable. But can we talk calmly now?"

"Yes."

"Good. My mother, your grandmother, took me to a place when she was quite old, and told me much the same as I am telling you. I said you were like a mirror of me, through time, to a younger age? Never has that been more true than today. Afterward, they said my mother had consumption, or some such word, but I think that was just something for them to say. I watched her walk on her spot, and then she died."

The young man rubbed his hands together, a useless nervous motion. The old man put his hand on his grandson's shoulder, a firm, assured gesture. He looked at the young man a long while and knew what to do. He stood and walked off slowly.

"Grandfather, please."

The old man turned back. "Grandson, I do not regret anything in life except for putting you through this grief today. You are a good man." He raised one hand, then turned and walked again.

The old man stepped onto the path and the path curved toward the light post. He took another step, and he fell, and his grandson raced to his side, but he was gone.

* * *

Several hours later, the young man sat upon the same bench, looking in the same direction. He watched the emergency crew take his grandfather away. He refused their offer of a ride, instead sitting for a while longer. Then he boarded the bus and took the reverse journey, back to the old man's home, alone. There, he tidied some things and finally turned the lights out and left, locking the door. He walked to the train station, then waited for a southbound train. They came less frequently at night, but one eventually came.

At the stop nearest his house, he left the train, exited the turnstile, and walked slowly up the stairs toward the street.

About the Author

The Fingers of the Colossus is my first collection of short stories, and only my second full-length published work. If you liked these stories, I urge you to leave a rating wherever you bought this book.

Leaving a rating is free and only takes a little of your time. You don't need to write anything too long — just a sentence or two telling what you thought of the story.

I'm an independent author who self-publishes his books. Ratings are just about the only thing that give my work legitimacy, and without them, the next potential reader may decide to read something else. So the two minutes you might spend leaving a review can have a lasting effect on my work and ensuring it continues.

And I'm going to be so bold as to ask you to do it *right now*, while the stories are still fresh in your mind. In a day or two, you may have other things to do, or forget what you wanted to say. So please, do it now.

If you enjoyed this collection, I hope you'll consider joining my mailing list where I can keep you updated on future books.

Finally, I'd love to hear from you. Drop me a line any time at ksoares@keithsoares.com

www.ingramcontent.com/pod-product-compliance
Lightning Source LLC
Chambersburg PA
CBHW020128180626
46810CB00004B/1449